BEST FRIENDS FOR NEVER

Also by Lisi Harrison:

THE CLIQUE

BEST FRIENDS FOR NEVER

A CLIQUE NOVEL BY
LISI HARRISON

LB 1837
LITTLE, BROWN AND COMPANY
New York Boston

Little, Brown and Company
Time Warner Book Group
1271 Avenue of the Americas, New York, NY 10020
Visit our Web site at www.lb-teens.com

First Edition

Produced by 17th Street Productions,
an Alloy company
151 West 26th Street, New York, NY 10001

10 9 8 7 6 5 4 3 2 1
CWO
Printed in the United States of America

Library of Congress Cataloging-in-Publication Data
Harrison, Lisi.
Best friends for never : a Clique novel / by Lisi Harrison.— 1st ed.
p. cm.
Summary: A bet about wardrobes between the wealthy Massie and middle-class Claire results in a testing of old friendships, a forging of new ones, and a change for the student body at Octavian Country Day School.
ISBN 0-316-70131-9
[1. Friendship—Fiction. 2. Cliques (Sociology)—Fiction. 3. Clothing and dress—Fiction. 4. Middle schools—Fiction. 5. Schools—Fiction. 6. Westchester (N.Y.)—Fiction.] I. Title. PZ7.H2527Be 2004
[Fic]—dc22

2004012501

For CeCe

Special Thanks

A very special thank-you to Ben Schrank, Lynn Weingarten, Les Morgenstein, and Josh Bank for your ongoing faith and guidance and for believing in me in that special way that's usually limited to family members. And to Lauren Levine and Deb Savo—the measure of a true friend is someone who reads more than five different versions of your first novel.

THE BLOCK ESTATE

DINING ROOM

7:45 PM

October 23rd

Massie Block hated herself for looking so beautiful. She angled a silver soup spoon toward her face and quickly glanced at her reflection. The new caramel-colored highlights in her dark hair brought out the amber flecks in her eyes and made them sparkle, just like her stylist, Jakkob, had promised. She was debuting a brown suede miniskirt that made her butt look even perkier than usual, and her arms and legs were lightly dusted with gold shimmer powder. Massie dropped the spoon and pushed it aside. She couldn't believe she was wasting this red-carpet outfit on her father's birthday dinner, especially since they were spending it at home with the Lyonses.

"Happy biiirthday, dear William, happy birthday to youuuuuu." The two families finished their song with a round of light applause. William's face turned purple as he struggled to blow out all forty candles at once, and Massie couldn't help giggling. It was the first time she had smiled all night.

They were seated around an elegant oak table in the Blocks' dining room, unable to fully see one another because of the elaborate centerpieces that overflowed with seasonal fruits and flowers. The teardrop-shaped bulbs on the crystal chandelier had been dimmed. The soft warm glow from the red candles was the room's main source of light.

Massie had been forced to sit between the two Lyons kids thanks to her mother's need to micromanage. On her left, Claire was shoveling a massive piece of sugary cake into her mouth as if *Cosmo* suddenly declared "fat" was the new "thin." Massie turned away. To her right was Todd, Claire's ten-year-old brother. Massie watched in disgust as he reached his icing-covered fingers over her plate to grab the pitcher of grape juice.

"Eew," Massie said under her breath.

She folded her thin arms tightly across her chest and shot her mother a sarcastic *thanks-a-lot* look. Kendra smiled back innocently. Massie rolled her eyes. But before her pupils could finish their journey, she was hit with a wave of grape juice that soaked the front of her skirt.

"Ehmagod!" Massie yelled. She pushed away from the table and jumped from her chair.

"Sorry." Todd shrugged his shoulders. "It was an accident."

He was fighting a smile and Massie knew he was lying.

"I swear, it's like you were raised by a pack of unbelievably dumb wolves," she said, dabbing her skirt with a white cloth napkin.

"Massie," Kendra snapped. She looked at Judi Lyons and shook her head apologetically.

Massie blushed. She realized her comment was more insulting to Todd's parents than to Todd but was too upset to apologize. If anyone should be saying "sorry," it was *them.* Ever since Labor Day, when the Lyons family left Orlando and moved into the Blocks' guesthouse, Massie's life had pretty much sucked. For the last two months Claire had been forcing herself on Massie. She crashed Massie's carpool, followed her around at school, and even tried to steal Massie's best friends. Lately Todd had been fighting for her attention too. The entire family was cramping her style and Massie was desperate to shake them. She hated that her dad chose to be "old college buddies" with Jay Lyons. Why couldn't he have picked Calvin Klein?

Todd grabbed a napkin and started rubbing Massie's skirt as if he was buffing the hood of a sports car.

"Lemme help you."

"Uchhh. Stay away from me, perv." Massie slapped his arm.

Massie saw her mother slide the diamond pendant back and forth on the platinum chain around her neck and shoot her husband a stern *do-something* look from across the table.

"Sweetie, relax," William said to his daughter. "Todd is only trying to help." His voice was firm and fatherly. "I'll buy you another skirt."

"But he did it on purpose," Massie said. "I saw him tilt the pitcher on me."

Kendra lifted the dainty china bell beside her dinner plate and shook it until Inez, the Blocks' live-in housekeeper, burst through the swinging door.

"Yes, Mrs. Block?" Inez smoothed the apron on her uniform, then cupped her hand around the tight gray bun on the back of her head. She liked everything in its proper place.

Kendra sighed and directed her gaze toward Massie.

Inez took one look at the stain and darted back into the

kitchen. She returned with a bottle of seltzer water and a sponge. Massie lifted her arms out to her sides and Inez started scrubbing as hard and fast as her bony arms would allow.

"Todd, did you do that on purpose?" Judi Lyons asked her son. She popped a chocolate-covered strawberry into her tiny mouth and did her best to chew it with her mouth closed.

"Of course he did," Massie screeched. "He's been staring at me with his big wet cow eyes ever since we sat down."

"Son, it looks like you're about as charming as your old man." Jay Lyons smacked his big belly and let out a hearty chuckle.

Todd kissed his fingertips and winked. Everyone laughed except Massie.

"Congratulations, Todd. You finally got me to notice you," Massie hissed. "What are you going to do tomorrow when I forget about you again? Blowtorch my bedroom?"

Claire took the napkin off her lap and threw it on her plate.

"Well, at least it's just an outfit, right?" Claire said. "It's not like you were hurt or anything."

"It's not 'just an outfit,' Kuh-laiiire." Massie pinched her skirt. *"This* is *suede."*

"Oh," Claire said. Then she chuckled to herself.

"What?" Massie snapped.

"I was just thinking how funny it is that, you know, clothes are sooo important to you. That's all."

"Actually, Claire, I find it 'funny' just how UN-important clothes are to *you.* You've worn that poo-colored turtleneck three days *this week.* And for some reason, you think those thick cords are for girls, when they're clearly for gangly dorks." Massie pointed to Todd. "You know, like your brother."

Massie moved away from Inez when she noticed how hard the woman was scrubbing. Chunks of yellow sponge had come off on her skirt. Massie was heartbroken. It was the most flattering skirt she had, and now it was destined to become a pillow for her black pug, Bean. She looked directly at Claire as if all of this was her fault.

"Hint, Claire. Next time you order your entire wardrobe from the J. Crew catalog, flip *past* the men's section," Massie said. "The women's clothes are always in the back."

"How would *you* know?" Claire said to her cords. "I thought you were *waaay* too fashionable to shop from a *cat-a-log.*" She said "catalog" the same way she'd say "snot sandwich."

"Hey, whaddaya say we all take a trip to the mall and buy you a new skirt? It'll be fun!" Judi Lyons clapped her pudgy hands and smiled as if she had just announced they were going to start celebrating Christmas five times a year.

Massie chugged her Pellegrino so she wouldn't have to respond to the offer. She couldn't imagine anything worse than having to wear something Judi Lyons picked out. The entire family dressed like tourists—oversized T-shirts, light wash denim, and sensible shoes.

"At least my *entire* life doesn't revolve around what people think of my outfits." Claire reached for the bobby pin that kept her overgrown bangs out of her eyes and slid it out of her blond hair. She gathered the pieces of hair that hung around her face and repinned them on the sides of her head.

"Hey, I thought we were supposed to be celebrating," Jay Lyons said. "Last time I checked, this was a birthday party." He pinched a piece of yellow cake off his plate and held it under the table for Bean.

Massie watched with satisfaction as her fit and trim puppy turned her tiny black nose up at the offer. She patted her thigh and Bean ran to her.

"Daddy, I didn't mean to ruin your party," Massie said to William. "It's just that I take *pride* in the way I look." She reached down and straightened the drooping turquoise feather boa around Bean's neck. "You taught me that, remember?"

"Of course I remember, honey," William said. "And you always look perfect to me."

"No thanks to him," Massie said, glaring at Todd.

Todd put his head in his hands and slowly rocked back and forth as if he was full of misery and regret. Massie knew he was faking, but Claire obviously had no clue.

"Massie, there is a difference between pride and obsession," Claire said. She put her arm around Todd's shoulders and continued. "Once you start screaming at ten-year-olds over a skirt, it's an obsession." Claire's hand trembled as she reached for her glass of soda.

The room was silent.

"Claire has a point, sweetie," Kendra said. She ran her fingers through her silky brown bob. "You haven't walked through the front door without a shopping bag since you were nine."

"That's not true." Massie put her hands on her hips and stood tall.

"It is," Claire said. "In the two months I've been here, you've gone shopping in New York City four times. And what about all of the after-school trips to the Westchester Mall?"

"Clothes are a necessity," Massie said. "I can't walk around naked, can I?"

"Says who?" Todd said with a devilish grin. "*I* think you can."

"Todd!" Judi snapped.

"He's just playing, dear," Jay said. "Aren't you, son?"

"No," Todd said. He winked at his father, who chuckled and shook his head.

Massie looked at Todd and rolled her eyes.

"You're a shopoholic," Claire said. "I bet you can't go an entire month without buying new clothes."

"Oh yeah? Well, you're a repeat offender. I bet you couldn't go an entire month without wearing the same outfit twice," Massie said. "Keds included."

"Massie!" Kendra and William exclaimed at the same time.

"Okay." Claire rose from her seat and stood to face Massie. "The first one to fold has to wear the other person's clothes to school for a week."

Massie's eyes widened with horror at the thought of having to wear high-waisted Gap jeans and sneakers to school.

"No way," Massie said. "You'd be lucky to wear my clothes. That's not a punishment—it's a reward. It's got to be something bad." Massie twirled the charm bracelet on her wrist while she thought. "I know, the loser has to wear one of my old snowsuits to class for a week. That includes leggings, goggles, ski boots, gloves, and a hat."

"Massie, you're being ridiculous," Kendra said.

Massie kept her focus on Claire.

"Fine," Claire agreed. She extended her arm and Massie grabbed Claire's hand. They shook over and over again, because neither one wanted to be the first to bow out and let go.

"This is great, Claire, thank you," William said with a playful smile. "You just saved me a ton of money."

The parents chuckled. But Claire and Massie's expressions didn't change. Their mouths were tightly pursed and both had a look of determination in their eyes.

Massie finally tore her hand away to answer her ringing cell phone. She lifted it out of the Louis Vuitton monogrammed case that was clipped to the belt on her skirt and walked out of the room. Bean followed.

"Hello?" Massie said. She was pacing around the cream-colored rug in the living room.

"Hey, it's Alicia. I have news that's worth at least ten gossip points."

Massie felt her heart speed up like it always did when she was about to hear gossip. She knew Alicia Rivera wasn't the type to ask for ten points unless she really deserved them. The Spanish beauty was a gossip expert and knew better than anyone that a decent piece usually earned about five points, max. This had to be big.

"Talk to me," Massie said. She sat down in the white wing chair beside the fireplace.

"I was in my golf class after school, right?"

"Right." Massie slipped out of the chair and started pacing again.

"And while we were stretching . . ."

"Yeah? Yeah? What?" Now she was bouncing on her toes.

"I heard Becca Wilder tell Liz Goldman that she thinks you are on your way *out.*"

"Out?" Massie barked at her reflection in the mirror over the mantel. "What do you mean, *out?*"

"Becca thinks that you're slipping and that you don't seem as in charge as you did last year."

"What did Liz say?"

"Liz agreed," Alicia said. "But that's nothing new. Liz always agrees with Becca. Anyway, they came up with the idea to throw an amazing boy-girl Halloween party so everyone would be talking about *them* and not you for a change. They even called it a Halloweenie party."

Massie was stunned. Her body felt frozen solid and burning hot at the same time. Her head was spinning.

Am I slipping? Are people starting to look at me as a popularity has-been? Why didn't I pick up on this sooner? Are Becca and Liz the only ones who think that, or is the whole grade over me? Why didn't I think of the boy-girl party? It should have been my idea. I always think of everything first!

"This can't be happening," Massie heard herself say. She

had meant to think it, but like everything these days, it hadn't worked out the way she had planned.

"If you want, I can have my dad's bodyguard scare the idea out of her," Alicia said with a soft giggle.

"No thanks, I'll do it myself," Massie said. "I'll show Becca and Liz and the rest of the grade that I'm not slipping. I gotta go." She was about to hang up when she realized Alicia was still on the line.

"Wait," Alicia asked. "What about the ten points?"

"This isn't about points, Alicia," Massie said. "It's about pride." And she snapped her phone shut.

Massie was about to walk back into the dining room but stopped when she heard her name. She crouched down behind the French doors so no one would see her and held her breath, trying not to miss a single word.

"I honestly don't know what it is with Massie and Claire," Judi said. "I thought they would be the best of friends by now."

Massie peered around the door to see Claire's reaction. But her seat was empty. She must have slipped out while Massie was on the phone.

"I agree with Judi," Kendra added. "I am so surprised."

"You don't look it," William said.

Kendra shrugged. "Botox."

"Just because they live on the same property doesn't mean they have to be joined at the hip," Jay said. "Maybe they need a little more time to adjust to each other. You know, like a couple of territorial house cats."

"Hissing cats would be a welcome change around here," Kendra said. She moved a half-eaten strawberry around her plate with a small silver dessert fork. "I've tried everything to bring them together. I am fresh out of ideas." She pushed her plate off to the side, moving the deep red herringbone place mat with it so the plate wouldn't scratch the glossy oak table.

Massie stood up quietly, holding the dangling charms on her bracelet so they wouldn't clang. She scooped up Bean and tiptoed up the stairs to her bedroom. She had a deliciously devious idea.

But before she did anything, Massie plopped down on her purple down-filled duvet and turned on her PalmPilot. Like other great historical figures, she had to sum up the latest events so future generations would have a record of her life.

CURRENT STATE OF THE UNION

IN	OUT
Shoporexic	Shopoholic
Halloweenie party	Chic-or-treating
Claire	Becca Wilder

THE GUESTHOUSE
CLAIRE'S BEDROOM
8:22 PM
October 23rd

Claire was in her bedroom, sitting at the dark mahogany secretary by her window. The antique desk came with the room, along with the rest of the dusty old furniture that had once belonged to Massie's grandmother.

"Okay, I know this is going to sound creepy," Claire said into the phone. "But my brother has a crush on Massie." She was talking to Layne Abeley, her first and only friend in Westchester.

"Isn't she a little old for him?" Layne asked.

"Not if he's looking for a babysitter."

Claire kicked off her white platform Keds and propped her legs up on the desk beside her unfinished fashion design homework. Even though FD was a required class at Octavian Country Day School, she had a hard time taking it seriously. How would an education in pattern making, sketching, sewing, and draping (whatever that was) possibly help her become a famous photographer? Her old school in Orlando would never offer a course about fashion. But then again, nothing about OCD reminded her of home.

"How was Mr. Block's birthday dinner?" Layne asked. She was chewing right into the phone, but Claire didn't mind. Layne's new favorite snack was popcorn and mustard, and lately she made almost constant crunching noises. Claire was just glad Layne had gotten over the oatmeal, her old favorite snack. Popcorn might be louder, but it was a lot less mushy.

Claire had begun filling Layne in on the bet she made with Massie when she was distracted by a *ding.* Someone had sent her an instant message.

MASSIEKUR: R U THERE?

Claire's insides froze. Massie's bedroom in the Block residence faced Claire's bedroom in the guesthouse, so there was a good chance she was being watched. Claire pushed her feet against the floor in a desperate attempt to slide her heavy leather upholstered chair away from the window.

Why did I open my big mouth during dinner?

"So wait," Layne said. "If you repeat *anything,* even shoes, you'll have to wear a snowsuit to school?"

"Yup."

"That's impossible. Why did you agree to that?"

"I'm tired of Massie thinking I'm a loser," Claire said, her voice drifting off. "I want to prove I can be just as tough as she is."

"Do you have *any* idea how many outfits are in a month?" Layne said.

Claire heard the rustling sound of a paper bag through the phone before getting an earful of Layne chewing her popcorn. It sounded like she was stomping on a pile of foam packing peanuts. Layne made a swallowing noise and then continued. "I'm sorry. That wasn't helpful. I'll bring you a bunch of clothes tomorrow."

"No, don't!" Claire said. Layne's latest obsession was secondhand old man pants and vintage concert tees. If Massie was embarrassed to be seen with Claire in this year's Gap, how would she ever take Claire seriously in Salvation Army?

"I'm sure Nurse Adele will be able to give me a few things from OCD's lost and found," Claire said. "Remember that great outfit she gave me when Alicia wiped red paint on my pants?"

"Yeah, but I have tons of great new clothes, so it's no problem," Layne said. "You'd do it for me, right?"

"Of course I would." Claire meant it.

"Hey, did you take the Smile Much quiz I e-mailed you?"

"Yeah," Claire said. She twirled the phone cord around her finger and wondered if she was the only person in Westchester younger than eighty-five who still used a land line.

"How did you do?"

Claire turned to her computer and clicked on the quiz.

"I only scored a fifteen. According to the results, that makes me a 'Mopey Dick.'"

"Why so low?" Layne asked. "I got a perfect thirty. According to the quiz, I'm 'Happy as a Clam.' What did you pick for number four?"

Claire scrolled down.

IF YOUR LIFE WAS A RIDE AT SIX FLAGS, IT WOULD BE . . .

(A) THE JESTER

(B) HURRICANE HARBOR

(C) THE SCREAM

"C." Claire sighed. "You?"

"A," Layne said. "What about the next one?"

Both girls read silently.

IF YOUR BEST FRIEND WAS ABDUCTED BY ALIENS, WHAT WOULD YOU MISS THE MOST?

(A) LAUGHING MY ABS OFF

(B) HANGING OUT WITH SOMEONE WHO GETS ME

(C) MISS?

"I picked A and B," Layne said. "I'd miss you for both reasons."

"Me too." Claire thought it was better to lie than to hurt Layne's feelings. If she had been with her Orlando friends, she would have answered A and B. But for now she picked C. She liked Layne but still secretly longed to be a part of Massie's fabulous foursome, just like everyone else at OCD. Massie, Alicia, Dylan, and Kristen went to every party in town and wore the coolest clothes, and everyone at school referred to them as the "Pretty Committee." So what if they threw smoked salmon at her a few weeks earlier? She would be willing to put it behind her if they would. Fitting in with them meant fitting in with *everyone,* and who wouldn't want that?

"What about the last one?" Layne said. "Once again I picked A."

Claire scrolled down to the final question.

THE HOT NEW GUY SITS BESIDE YOU IN SCIENCE LAB (OMG!). HOW DO YOU DEAL?

(A) INVITE HIM TO EXPERIMENT WITH YOU AFTER SCHOOL

(B) FLASH HIM THAT "COME-HITHER" SMILE YOU'VE BEEN PRACTICING IN THE BATHROOM MIRROR. THEN WAIT FOR HIS MOVE

(C) SWITCH SCHOOLS. HE'S MORE DISTRACTING THAN A *REAL WORLD* MARATHON

"What difference does it make?" Claire said. "It's not like we even *have* boys at our school." She wound the phone cord tightly around her index finger and watched her skin turn from pink to purple.

"Easy, Mopey Dick," Layne teased.

"All of my Florida friends have been e-mailing me about their latest crushes. Meanwhile, the only Westchester guy I've been hanging out with is Mr. Block. Don't you ever want to meet cute guys and have crushes and get all nervous when they're around?"

"No," Layne said. "I try not to want anything—that way I'm never disappointed."

"How is it possible not to want anything? What about that color printer you keep talking about?"

"It doesn't apply to merchandise."

Claire heard a loud snap.

"Ow!" Layne said. "I think that kernel just broke my tooth."

DING.

MASSIEKUR: DESPR8

"You okay?" Claire tried to stay focused on her conversation with Layne, but Massie was obviously determined to get her attention. Massie was switching her desk lamp on and off so quickly, Claire thought her room looked like it was caught in a severe electrical storm.

"Layne, can you hold on for a second?"

Phone in hand, Claire slid off her slippery leather chair and landed under her desk. If she was going to keep ignoring Massie's cries for help, she would have to take cover. She couldn't believe she had been reduced to hiding from Massie in her own house. It was *beyond* embarrassing.

Claire moved her hand across the bottom of the windowsill until she found the bottoms of the heavy beige curtains. She gripped them between her index and middle fingers and slid them shut.

"'Kay, I'm back, sorry 'bout that." Claire peered out from under the desk at the round chunky legs on her four-poster bed. They looked like something straight out of a knight's castle. An ivory lace runner hung over the top of her dark dresser drawers and made her think of old ladies. All of the furniture in her room looked tired and unfriendly, like it would much rather be somewhere else. She missed the bright modern bedroom she left behind in Florida and made a mental note to ask her mother if she could remove the yellowed photographs of the Blocks' dead relatives so she could put up some of her own shots.

"I want to find a boyfriend." Claire sighed. "Maybe then my life won't seem so pathetic."

"You can't expect someone else to make you happy," Layne said. Then she launched into a speech about boys and how much trouble they could be, but Claire was too distracted to pay attention. Someone wearing a pair of black pointy-toed boots was standing in front of her desk, tapping her foot. Claire's heart started to pound.

"Layne, I have to finish my design homework. I'll see you tomorrow in class," Claire said. She yanked on the phone cord until the beige base fell off her desk and landed on the floor in front of her. She pulled it toward her and quickly hung up.

"Why were you ignoring me?"

Claire craned her neck out from under the desk and looked up. Massie stood above her with her hands on her hips. She was snapping her Dentyne Ice.

"I have no idea what you're talking about. I've been down here for like the last ten minutes, looking for my earring."

"When did you get your ears pierced? After dinner?"

"Is this about the bet?" Claire asked. "Are you mad?"

"No. I welcome the challenge. Now get up." Massie offered her hand. Claire took it.

The crown charm on Massie's bracelet dug into Claire's palm, but she didn't dare complain.

Once they were face-to-face, Massie spoke.

"Claire," Massie said. Her voice was suddenly sweet. "Remember a few weeks ago you said you wished your parents would let you have a cell phone?"

"Yeah . . ."

"Well, I know how you can get it." Massie started pacing. "From now on, all we have to do is act like we're best friends and our moms will give us anything we want."

"What are you talking about?" Claire asked.

"I overhead them talking about how badly they want us to get along, sooo, all we have to do is give them what they want and we'll get what *we* want." Massie flashed a proud smile.

"But how—?"

"Look, you want a cell phone and I want a boy-girl Halloween party. Follow my lead and they're as good as ours."

Claire weighed the options. If she agreed, Massie would be grateful, which could lead to friendship down the line. She'd also get a cell phone, which would definitely help her fit in around school. And she'd finally have the opportunity to meet some Briarwood boys at the party and find a crush. Her days as "Mopey Dick" would be behind her forever.

"Okay," Claire said. "Let's do it."

THE BLOCK ESTATE
THE LIVING ROOM
9:00 PM
October 23rd

"Stop acting so scared," Massie said. She smacked Claire's hand away from her mouth, putting an end to the irritating nail-biting sounds. "You're acting like you've never lied to your parents before."

Claire was about to respond but was silenced by Massie's palm.

"Shhh."

They were pressed up against the leopard print wall-paper just outside the living room, waiting for the perfect time to interrupt their parents' conversation.

"What about *The Producers?*" Kendra asked her husband. "You liked that play."

"No, dear, I said I didn't *hate* it."

"Well, I hated it," Jay said.

"You hate anything that doesn't take place on a football field," Judi said.

Massie looked at Claire and rolled her eyes. She couldn't believe their parents talked about such boring things.

"Okay, we're going in," Massie said. "Remember, even if something I say sounds strange, go with it." Then she grabbed Claire by the elbow and pulled her forward into the room.

"Hey, everyone." Massie squeezed Claire's arm.

"Hey," Claire said, right on cue.

Massie took a deep breath. The familiar smell of coffee and burning wood filled the air. Massie instantly relaxed. She had worked this room a thousand times.

"Claire and I just wanted to say happy birthday to Dad one more time before we went to bed," Massie said.

"Y-yeah, happy birthday, William," Claire added. Her voice was strained and her smile forced.

"Wanna ask them?" Massie turned to Claire. She knew Claire would have no idea what she was talking about and hoped she would play along.

"No, you should," Claire said. "You're such a good asker."

"Thanks." Massie looked at Claire with a humble smile and puppy dog eyes, hoping her parents would believe affection and respect flowed effortlessly between them.

"Mom, Dad, Judi, Jay," she addressed her audience. "Claire and I were talking before bed, which we've been doing *ah lot* lately, and—" She paused for effect.

Claire nodded in agreement.

Massie continued. "We were thinking about maybe having a Halloween party at the house this year."

Massie looked for her mother's reaction first, because it was the only one that mattered. Kendra presided over all things related to the house, school (before, during, and after), spending money, sleepovers, punishments, and food. Her dad only stepped in when it came to grades, curfews, and loud music that needed to be turned down.

Kendra had a delicate white mug with gold trim raised

to her lips but put it down before taking a sip. The clink of the china was the only sound in the room. Massie couldn't stand the silence and rushed to fill it.

"Of course, we would stay in the backyard so the house doesn't get dirty," she added quickly. "Oh, and Claire has a great idea. Wait till you hear it."

Massie knew it was crucial for her parents to think that she and Claire had spent hours discussing this and that saying no to the party would be like saying no to their first steps toward friendship.

"Go on," Massie said. "Tell 'em."

Claire stared right back at Massie and asked, "Whhhat?" through her teeth. It came out sounding like, "Ahhht?"

"Ehmagod, you are sooo modest." Massie put her arm around Claire. "*She* thought it would be cool to invite a few boys to the party, too. You know, just to balance things out and to get some interesting costumes in the mix."

Massie discreetly pressed her arm down on Claire's shoulder, reminding her to play along. Claire brushed her hand against the back of Massie's leg to say that she would.

"Claire, that was *your* idea?" Judi asked. She sounded pleasantly surprised.

"Looks like our little Lyon is one big dog," Jay replied, and followed up with a phlegmy laugh.

"Don't tease." Judi slapped her husband's arm playfully. "I think it's perfectly normal that she's ready to interact with boys."

Massie could feel Claire starting to squirm under her arm.

"So Mom, can I?" Massie asked.

"Can you what?"

"Can I have the party?"

"Can *you* have the party?" Kendra looked from Massie to Claire and then back to Massie again.

Massie's mouth dried up and a rush of prickly heat shot up the back of her neck.

How could I make such a stupid mistake?

"I assumed you two were going to co-host." Kendra tapped the side of her mug with her bloodred acrylic nail tips.

"Especially since it was *Claire's* idea to have the boys in the first place," Judi said. She leaned in toward the dessert tray on the coffee table, snapped off a piece of biscotti, and popped it in her mouth.

"Oh, we're definitely co-hosts," Massie said. "We've already started working on our list."

"I hope your brother, Todd, is in on it," Jay said to Claire.

"Of course he is." Claire stuffed her hands into the side pockets of her cords.

"And how many kids did you plan to invite from your grade?" Kendra asked her daughter.

Massie paused. If she said "everyone," her mom might worry about noise or mess. But if she said "almost everyone," her mother would be angry she was leaving people out.

"Everyone," Massie said, deciding that when it came to her mother, it was always best to include. She held her breath while she waited for a reaction.

"We'll sleep on it," Kendra answered.

Massie stomped her foot and put her hands on her hips.

"I need to know—" Massie felt Claire tap her on the back of the leg. "I mean, *we* need to know tonight," she said. "Halloween is only a week away, and we want to get Landon Dorsey to plan it."

"Who?" Claire asked.

"She's the best party planner in the entire 914 area code. There is *nothing* that woman can't do," Massie said.

Kendra looked at the girls one last time and sighed. "I'm okay with it if you are," she said to the other parents.

"Have Landon call me with the cost," William said.

"Thanks, Daddy." Massie ran over to the couch. She hugged her father and planted a big kiss on his balding head.

"What about the cell phone?" Claire whispered to Massie.

"Huh?" Massie said. She was busy massaging her father's shoulders.

"You told me you'd help me ask for a cell phone."

Massie started karate chopping William's back.

"Honey," Jay said to Claire. "You know the rule. NO cell phones until you're sixteen."

"I know." Claire looked down at her fluffy pink slippers.

"Well, g'nite," Massie said, her voice bursting with cheer. She kissed her parents and headed off to bed.

Claire ran out after her.

Todd was sitting on the hardwood floor outside the living room, playing his Game Boy on mute so he could eavesdrop.

"Hey, Massie, how 'bout for the party I dress up as a rock star and you can go as my stalker?"

"Hey, Todd," Massie said. "How 'bout you dress up as a roadside raccoon and I'll go as a speeding truck driver?"

"Are you serious?" Todd asked Massie. "I love that."

Massie ignored him and was speeding toward the stairs when she saw that Claire had followed her out of the room.

"I can't believe you tricked me like that!" Claire shouted at Massie. "I thought we had a deal."

"Then DEAL!" Massie shouted back.

"Good one!" Todd slapped his hand against his faded jeans. "Hey, who wants to make root beer floats?"

But all he got in return were heavy sighs, stomping feet, and slamming doors.

HARDAPPLE ORCHARDS

HAYRIDE

11:15 AM

October 24th

The rickety Hardapple Orchards wagon jerked and wobbled as it rolled over the clumps of hay and horse poo that covered the trails. The entire seventh-grade class struggled to keep their hot chocolate from spilling all over the rough wool blankets that covered them. Massie fixed her gaze on the passing apple trees and thought about how she'd get back at Becca Wilder.

It was their second field trip of the year, and despite the chilly air and the bumpy ride, it was going much better than the first.

"Hey, Kristen," Britton Daniels shouted toward the back of the wagon. "You're not going to be selling any bad makeup on *this* trip, are you?"

Britton and her B-list friends giggled.

Massie saw Kristen clench her jaw muscles.

"Don't let her get to you," Massie said. "How were you supposed to know the makeup would make everyone's lips swell up?"

"Yeah," Dylan Marvil said. "It's not *your* fault they got rushed to the hospital." She twirled a piece of long red hair around her index finger.

"Dylan's right." Alicia's beautiful almond-shaped eyes

looked hazel in the sunlight. "It's their fault for having sensitive skin."

Despite the comforting words of her best friends, Kristen refused to let it go.

"Hey, Medusa," Kristen fired back. "This time I thought I'd sell you something from my new line of power tools. Maybe an electric saw will help you comb through that lice trap you call your hair."

Britton ran her hand across the back of her head. Massie, Alicia, and Dylan roared with laughter.

"That's enough, girls," Heidi said. Their nature-loving science teacher was zigzagging her way over to Kristen, clutching onto her students for balance as she passed. When she finally reached her target, Heidi rested her palm on Kristen's shoulder and continued her lesson.

"We will be at the pumpkin patch in a few minutes. In ancient Greece pumpkins were called *pepons,* which is Greek for 'large melon.'" The turbulent wagon made her voice shake.

"That's a nice pair of *pepons* you got there," Massie whispered to Alicia.

Alicia was super-sensitive about her big boobs and Massie knew it. But she wasn't about to pass up the opportunity for a good joke.

Alicia responded by smacking Massie on the arm as hard as she could.

Dylan laughed out loud, but it was Kristen's cackle that caught their teacher's attention.

"One more interruption and there will be no pumpkin picking for you today," Heidi said to Kristen.

Kristen lifted the wide collar of her turtleneck over her blushing face and hid.

The horse-drawn cart rolled up to a huge pumpkin patch and Farmer Randy pulled the reins until they came to a complete stop. Heidi started explaining how the pumpkins' bright orange color came from beta-carotene, but the girls had already tuned her out. Most of them were too busy scanning the orchard so they could outpick each other when they were finally let loose.

"Someone should tell these losers that they can buy pumpkins for twenty bucks on every corner in our neighborhood," Massie said.

"What? And ruin all their fun?" Alicia put her hand on her heart and shook her head to show she pitied her naive classmates.

The second Heidi unlatched the wooden gate on the side of the wagon, the "losers" busted out like stampeding bulls. Claire and Layne held hands and laughed hysterically while they ran, moving as fast as their matching steel-toed hiking boots could take them, which wasn't very fast at all. Layne's friends Meena and Heather ran along beside them.

Massie, Alicia, Dylan, and Kristen trailed behind. They had no interest in pumpkins, picking, or soil.

"Wanna know what we're doing this year for Halloween?" Massie asked.

"Hmmm, lemme guess," Dylan said. "Trick-or-treating,

eating fistfuls of candy, gaining five pounds, and then eating nothing but Slim Fast shakes for a week?"

"Nope," Massie said. "This year we're going to do something totally different."

"Ehmagod." Alicia stopped dead in her tracks and turned to face Massie. Kristen and Dylan stopped too but weren't exactly sure why.

"You're gonna beat Becca to the boy-girl party, aren't you?"

Massie responded with a cocky half smile and a nod.

Dylan and Kristen jumped up and down with excitement. And soon all four of them were bouncing together in a giddy huddle shouting, "Hello, weenie!" over and over again.

"I can't wait to see the look on Becca's face when she hears the news," Dylan said.

"Why wait?" Massie said. "Let's tell her now."

Becca and Liz were only a few feet away. The two muscular gymnasts were surrounded by a group of girls who were cheering as they struggled to lift their massive pumpkin off the ground.

Becca was dressed in one of her usual girly chiffon tops, which always looked out of place on her stocky physique. Her dirty blond shoulder-length hair hung flat and lifeless around her oval face. Massie and the rest of the Pretty Committee had once decided if it weren't for her piercing blue eyes, no one would look at her twice.

Liz was a petite version of Becca, without the eyes. Hers were a dull shade of brown. People noticed Liz because she was constantly orange from her addiction to spray tanning.

"I can't tell where that pumpkin ends and Liz begins," Massie said.

Alicia, Dylan, and Kristen cracked up as they tiptoed toward their targets so their heels wouldn't get stuck in the mud.

"Hey, Becca," Massie shouted.

"Hey." Becca took off her Kangol cap and fluffed up her hair. "Did you come to check out my pumpkin? It's so big, Farmer Randy went to get a wheelbarrow so we can get it on the wagon."

"No, I came over to tell you the meaning of life," Massie said. Kristen, Dylan, and Alicia snickered.

"What are you talking about?" Liz asked. "Nobody knows the meaning of life."

"Massie does." Alicia sat down on Becca's pumpkin and kicked her leg back and forth, each time denting it a little more with the heel of her boot.

"What are you doing?" Becca screeched. "Get off that."

"Puh-lease, I'm not even touching it."

The girls who had been watching Becca and Liz wrestle the pumpkin took a few steps back. They didn't want to get involved.

"So, what is the meaning of life?" Liz asked.

"I'm having a boy-girl party for Halloween," Massie replied.

"No way!" Becca screeched. She stomped her foot in the dirt. "That's not fair. That was *my* idea."

"THAT'S LIFE!" Massie, Kristen, Alicia, and Dylan shouted

at the same time. They finished rubbing it in with a round of high fives.

The girls on the sidelines giggled into their hands.

Becca was stunned.

"Do something," Liz mouthed to her.

But before Becca could do anything, there was a loud *pop*. Becca whipped her head around in search of the source.

"Oops." Alicia's big brown eyes were wide as she feigned surprise. "Sorry." She jumped to the ground and pointed to her Jimmy Choo boot sticking out of the pumpkin.

Alicia stood on one foot and tugged at the heel while Kristen and Dylan held the pumpkin down to keep it from rolling over.

"I can't believe you did that." Becca's bottom lip twitched as she fought back tears.

The girls in the background giggled again.

"Let's tell Heidi," Liz said.

"No, don't," Becca said, grabbing her friend by the arm. She knew better than to tell.

"Got it!" Alicia pulled the boot free. She wiped the slimy orange guts off the heel and smeared them on the side of the pumpkin.

"Are you really having a boy-girl Halloween party?" Becca asked.

"Wait, Becca," Liz chimed in. "Maybe hers isn't on the thirty-first." She clearly thought she was on to something.

Even Becca rolled her eyes when she heard that one.

"Unless the date of Halloween has officially changed, mine is on the thirty-first," Massie said. "But since you think that I'm, quote, *slipping,* end quote, and that I'm, quote, not in charge like I used to be, end quote, don't count on an invite."

Massie, Alicia, Dylan, and Kristen turned and walked off, leaving two mortified girls, their shocked friends, and one mangled pumpkin behind them.

"Come on, ladies," Heidi shouted. She was standing two rows away pointing excitedly at a pile of miniature *pepons,* as if *that* would suddenly inspire them to participate.

"Pretend you're deaf," Massie said. They ignored the teacher and changed directions at the same time.

"So, what exactly goes on at a boy-girl party?" Dylan asked. She tried to sound interested instead of nervous, but Massie saw right through her.

"It's one big make-out session," Massie said. "Only at my party everyone will be in costumes, so we won't even know who we're making out with."

"Are you serious?" Kristen asked.

"Are you stupid?" Massie shot back. "I'm kidding."

"Actually, it *is* kind of like that." Alicia tossed her long dark hair over her shoulder.

"What?" Massie, Dylan, and Kristen all asked at the same time.

"I went to a boy-girl at my cousin's this summer in Spain, and we played Kiss or Be Kissed for like five hours." Alicia rolled back her shoulders and stood confidently before them. They stared back blankly.

"What?" Alicia asked. "You've never played K or B K'ed?"

"Are you going to tell us what it is?" Massie snapped. She hated it when one of her friends knew more than she did.

"Basically, when it's your turn, you have to pick someone to kiss. And if you don't, the person beside you makes the decision for you." Alicia paused. "I kissed so many boys, by the end of the night I'd gone through an entire tube of lip gloss."

Massie had no idea how to respond. She suddenly felt like her best friend was a total stranger.

"Well, I'm not sure if that game will fly with my mom, but we can try," Massie said. For the first time in her life, she hoped her mother would be around to meddle.

Massie noticed Kristen and Dylan staring at her, trying to read her expression. She didn't want them to know she was secretly panicking too, so she turned toward the nearest pumpkin and kicked it.

"This one's not quite ripe yet," she said to no one in particular.

"I say we wear really sexy costumes," Alicia suggested.

"I'm all for that." Dylan twirled around to show off her new trim waistline and got smacked in the face by her own wavy red hair as she spun. "Seven days and I've already lost five pounds on the South Beach Diet. I'm going to look like a supermodel by Halloweenie."

"I'll need an unsexy costume to wear to the party or my parents won't let me out of the house," Kristen said.

Alicia turned around and aimed her big brown eyes right at Kristen.

"Why don't we make it a 'Be Yourself' party and you can go as a nun?"

"Does that mean you'll be going as a bitch or a slut?" Kristen shot back.

"Both," Alicia said with a mischievous grin.

"Just because my parents are total prudes doesn't mean I am. Besides, I want to be sexy in case Derrick Harrington is there." Kristen's face turned bright red when she said the boy's name. "You're inviting him, right, Mass?"

"Given."

"When did you start liking Derrick Harrington?" Dylan asked. She sat down on a big pumpkin and crossed her legs.

"I've had a crush on him for the last few weeks," Kristen said. "Since the OCD benefit."

The annual black-tie auction took place at Massie's house every September. It was the community's way of raising money for the local private school, but more importantly, it was an opportunity to flirt with boys. That night Massie had developed a secret crush on Cam Fisher. He was part of the A-list group at Briarwood and was known for being an ah-mazing soccer goalie. But Massie was more impressed that he knew the words to every song they danced to. That night Massie decided not to tell her friends about her crush until she could be absolutely sure Cam liked her back. She was hoping the Halloween party would give her the answers she was looking for.

"Massie, I told you I liked Derrick Harrington, remember?" Kristen asked.

"No way." Dylan rolled her eyes. "I told Massie that I liked him first."

"No, you told *me,*" Alicia said.

"Oh," Dylan replied. "And you didn't tell Kristen? I'm shocked."

"I didn't need the points that week. I had already hit twenty."

"Whatever. I thought it was obvious. I mean, we danced *all* night."

"Yeah, but you said he moved like he was getting electrocuted," Kristen said.

"Well, you said he was too short for you and all he wanted to talk to you about was soccer," Dylan replied.

"Which is a good thing, since I LOVE SOCCER," Kristen said.

"Why don't you let Derrington decide who he likes," Massie said. She smiled to herself for coming up with "Derrington," because it was a total soap opera name. How appropriate, considering the drama.

"Fine," Kristen and Dylan both said.

"Not that either one of you would know what to do with him if you got him," Alicia teased.

Both girls scowled at Alicia and then at each other.

"Now can we please stop fighting and start talking about our costumes?" Massie hated when her friends fought. The thought of her group splitting petrified her. Not only would school be boring if they couldn't hang out together, but then Becca would be right. Massie wouldn't be in charge anymore. Her friends were her strength, and without all three of them she would start to slip.

Heidi blew her whistle, which signaled it was time to get back on the wagon.

Massie, Kristen, and Alicia grabbed the first pumpkins they saw, and Dylan picked up a tiny, bumpy gourd. The girls roared with laughter at Dylan's last-minute choice, and for a moment their fighting seemed like a thing of the past.

They boarded the wagon and reclaimed their seats in the back.

"I gave it a lot of thought last night, and I think we should be Dirty Devils," Massie continued. "That way we can be dirty and evil at the same time."

"That's a great idea," Dylan said. She popped four pieces of bubble gum in her mouth at once. Massie knew this meant Dylan was still upset.

"Yeah, I love it," Alicia joined in.

"What exactly does that mean?" Kristen asked.

"Well, for the dirty part we'll wear tight shredded T-shirts so it looks like we've been in a bunch of pitchfork battles and red microminis with black Calvin boy shorts underneath," Massie said. "And then we'll have tails and horns for the devil part."

"Ooh, we should write messages on the back of the boy shorts so everyone can read them," Alicia said.

"Yeah, in glitter," Dylan added.

"I was gonna say that," Kristen said.

Dylan rolled her eyes.

When Farmer Randy pulled into the parking lot, Dylan leaned across Massie and Alicia and plunked her bumpy gourd on Kristen's lap.

"Since you want *everything* that's mine, you might as well have this too," she said.

"Don't mind if I do," Kristen said. She stuffed the comma-shaped fruit in her bag.

CURRENT STATE OF THE UNION

IN	OUT
Massie Block	Becca Wilder/Liz Goldman
Fighting over boys	Fighting over toys
Gourds	Pumpkins

Carpool with Layne Abeley

Backseat

3:35 PM

October 24th

Layne leaned across the backseat of her parents' Lexus and whispered in Claire's ear.

"I can't believe you're inviting *boys* to the party."

"Why are you whispering?" Claire asked.

Layne gestured toward her mother, who was in the front seat, driving carpool.

"If she hears we're hanging out with boys, she'll start asking us who we like and it will be totally embarrassing," Layne said. "Trust me."

"And *that's* why you don't want them at the party?" Claire said.

"No. I just think the party won't be fun now, that's all."

Claire turned to look out the window. Fall had come and the trees were almost bare—just a few yellow and red leaves were still holding on. Claire had never experienced the different seasons in Orlando and hoped this one would bring some much needed change to her social life.

After a brief moment of silence, Claire looked back at Layne.

"Everyone will be trying to act all cool to impress the boys, and no one will be themselves," Layne said.

"I think guys will make the party better," Claire said.

"My old school was coed and everything seemed much easier than it does at OCD. For one thing, boys don't fight half as much as girls and they have other things to talk about besides clothes."

"I think this party is an excuse for Massie and her friends to show off. How much do you wanna bet they'll dress up as cats or Playboy bunnies or French maids just so they can look hot?"

Claire turned her entire body to face Layne's. "Have you ever gone to school with boys?" she asked.

Layne leaned over the driver's seat and rested her chin on her mother's arm.

"Mom, did my nursery school have boys?"

"Yes," her mother answered. "Now get your head off me before I get into an accident."

Layne sighed and flopped back in her seat.

"See," Claire said. "You have no experience. That's why you're scared."

"What *experience* do *you* have?" Layne whispered. "Have you ever gone on a date?"

"Who needs a date?" Claire whispered back. "Recess three times a day with boys can teach a girl a lot."

Finally Claire could say she had done something no one else at OCD had, even if it was just playing tag with boys during recess and getting her hair pulled in class. She intended on milking her so-called experience as much as she could.

Mrs. Abeley pulled the car into the circular driveway of the Block estate.

"Thanks for the ride, Mrs. Abeley." Claire winked at Layne before she stepped out of the Lexus. "I'll call you later," she whispered.

Claire made extra sure to close the door gently behind her. One of the many lessons she had learned from Westchester's elite was never to slam a car door. Apparently it was a heinous crime, as heartless as kicking a puppy.

Judi Lyons drove up right behind her. She rolled down her window and lowered the volume on the car stereo that had been blasting Kelly Clarkson.

"Claire, will you help me unload the groceries?"

Claire watched the Abeleys' luxury car round the circular driveway and glide away from the Block estate. She turned back to her mother.

"When are you and Dad going to get a *real* car?" Claire asked. "Aren't you tired of driving around in this ugly Ford Taurus rental?"

"Since when have you started paying attention to cars?" Judi looked at her daughter with a trace of suspicion in her eyes. She handed Claire two bags of groceries.

"I'm curious, that's all. I think you and Dad deserve something *better.*"

Claire stopped walking and lowered the heavy bags onto the driveway. She readjusted her grip and lifted them again.

"Better than a Taurus?" Judi said. "Why waste the money? This car is perfect for us. Anyway, I thought you loved it."

"I did," Claire said. "I just think it's time for a change."

"Well, when *you* can afford something better, let me know," Judi said.

Claire was too ashamed to answer and wished she had never brought it up.

They carried the bags into the kitchen and set them down on the white Formica breakfast table.

"Thanks for your help. I'll unpack them," Judi said. "Don't you have a party planning meeting?"

"Yeah, it's at four o'clock," Claire said. "I still have fifteen minutes."

After inhaling two bowls of Cap'n Crunch, Claire headed over to the main house. According to her pink Baby G-Shock, she was five minutes early. She rang the doorbell three times, hoping to get a few minutes of costume talk with Massie before Landon arrived.

"Claire, I'm glad you finally made it," Kendra said while she took Claire's coat. "Massie and Landon are waiting for you in the sunroom."

The hallway was warm and toasty compared to the crisp October air, and Claire felt her cheeks tingling as they thawed. A Thanksgiving smell filled the house. This was thanks to Inez, who was in the kitchen preparing dinner—crispy chicken, twice-baked potatoes, pecan pie, and frozen yogurt for Massie. Claire slipped off her sneakers and made her way to the "greenhouse." Three walls were made of glass and faced the backyard. But instead of plants and flowers, it was filled with a pool table and a stocked bar.

"Massie, are you familiar with the word *jux-ta-po-si-tion*?"

Claire heard a woman ask. The stranger pronounced every letter and every syllable she spoke, like she sharpened her words with knives before she used them. "Because that's what I'm going for here. The instant you place two opposites beside each other, or jux-ta-pose them, you get magic. This is why I think the theme of your party should be—"

Her sentence came to a screeching halt when Claire entered the room.

"Oh, you started already?" Claire asked. "It's just four o'clock now."

"Speaking of opposites," Landon hissed. She lifted her thick black-rimmed glasses and examined Claire's outfit.

"I said three forty-five," Massie said. "But it's no big deal. I already filled her in."

Claire sighed. She reached into the back pocket of her old khakis. She never would have worn such snug pants if it wasn't for her bet with Massie. Every time she pulled down her pants to pee, she noticed the imprint of the waistband on her stomach. Of course Massie's outfit was perfect—black tights, pleated denim mini, and a fluffy cashmere cowl-neck.

Twenty-nine days to go.

"It says four o'clock on this note you left for me last night." Claire pulled out a folded piece of paper and held it out in front of her.

Massie shrugged.

"Wipe that befuddled look off your puss," Landon said. "And come join us. You're already late enough as it is." She patted the empty bar stool beside her.

Claire sat down. Landon smoothed her manicured hand over the top of her head, making sure the interruption hadn't caused any hairs to pop out of her tight chignon. "As I was saying, the perfect theme for your event is When Hell Freezes Over." She clapped and held her hands in a prayer position, waiting for the girls' reactions. She got nothing but blank stares.

"You know, like fire and ice. Together," Landon said.

"I love it," Massie said. "Can we build a skating rink?"

"We can do anything you want." Landon drew her stylus like a sword and started tapping the screen of her PalmPilot while she rattled off some last-minute thoughts.

"I'll need fifteen podiums, twenty severed heads, seven waitresses dressed like Satan, mannequins . . . preferably foam, a DJ, and at least five pitchforks for every bonfire pit, which I will call . . . hmmm, what will I call them?"

Landon tapped the stylus against her chin while she thought. "I know . . . The Pits of Despair. Too genius!" She looked up and noticed the girls staring at her.

"Well," she continued as she powered down her organizer. "I can probably finish up at my office."

Claire breathed a sigh of relief.

"Oops, one more thing." Landon pulled a box out of her bag. "I brought invitations for you. If you don't like the scaredy cats, I have ghosts in the car."

"It's okay, the cats are good." Massie reached for the box. "Ghosts are so sixth grade."

"Agreed," Landon said.

"Will there be candy?" Claire asked. She didn't care about waitresses or podiums or scaredy cats. The only things she wanted at this party were boys and treats.

"Excuse me?" Landon turned her head slowly to face Claire.

"I was just wondering if there was going to be can-dee?" Claire asked.

"Ignore her," Massie instructed Landon. "It's her first event."

Landon pulled a shiny gold business card out of a case and handed it to Claire.

"What does it say under the name Landon Dorsey?" she asked.

Claire looked at Massie. Massie shrugged.

Claire looked at the business card.

"It says 'professional party planner.'"

"Right," Landon said. Her eyes were closed. "Which means there will be enough candy to keep you puking until I'm back to plan your sweet sixteen."

And with that Landon gathered her things and tossed her lipstick-covered Starbucks cup in the trash.

"Get started on those invites," she called over her shoulder. "I want them in the mail tomorrow morning. The party is a week away."

"'Kay," they both shouted back.

"Terminator," Claire said under her breath. "I can't believe you *like* her. I was waiting for her to take her face off and show us her wires and dangling eyeballs."

"She'z ah prafeshhhanal pahtee planna," Massie said, doing her best Arnold impersonation.

Claire was shocked. She'd expected Massie to rush to Landon's defense.

"She'll be beck when we-ya zixteen," Claire joined in.

Both girls busted out laughing.

"She's a total freak, but she's good," Massie said. "You just have to trust her and not ask stupid questions like if there will be *candy* at a Halloween party."

Claire let out a heavy sigh. Her moment of fun with Massie was over.

"Here's a list of all of the seventh-grade OCD girls and the Briarwood boys." Massie opened her lavender Clairefontaine notebook and placed it on the bar so Claire could see it. The she reached into her black messenger bag and pulled out a bottle of purple nail polish. "I'll write out the invites for the boys since none of them know you yet, and I'll also cover everyone I mark with a purple dot. You can do everyone else. 'Kay?"

Claire noticed *her* list was made up of all the girls Massie had once referred to as the LBR (Losers Beyond Repair).

"Who's this?" Claire asked, pointing to the purple question mark Massie had painted beside one of the names.

"Olivia Ryan," Massie said. "She's a total airhead. No one's seen her since school started. Knowing her, she probably forgets where it is." Massie tapped the bottle of nail polish against her bottom teeth. "She'll go on my list."

Massie dabbed a drop of purple over the question mark

beside Olivia's name and replaced it with a check. "Oh, and remember," she said. "Put Claire Lyons and *your* phone number where it says RSVP so the people you're inviting know to call *you* and not me."

Later that night, Claire did exactly what she was told. Only she decided to spell her name *M-a-s-s-i-e B-l-o-c-k* and include a certain someone's cell phone number with special instructions to "call anytime day or night."

Claire knew Massie would probably force her to eat lunch in the musty janitor's closet for a month when she found out. But it was worth it. She was tired of being treated like a loser.

"If you can't join 'em, beat 'em." Claire licked her last envelope and sealed it shut.

THE BLOCK ESTATE
MASSIE'S BEDROOM
11:45 AM
October 25th

Massie stood in front of her full-length mirror and tilted her head to the right. She always did this when she tried on a new outfit. The off-center angle helped her see what she looked like through someone else's eyes. It was the closest thing she had to a second opinion.

"Ugh, I can't wear this either," Massie said to Bean, who was curled up in a tiny ball on a hill of sweaters. She pulled a red V-neck over her head and tossed it on the bed with the rest of her rejects. Normally, the fluffy purple duvet was the only burst of color in Massie's all-white room. But today clothes in every color were in plain view. Massie put her hands on her hips and evaluated the mess.

"It looks like my closets all barfed at the same time. This bet is a nightmare."

Bean opened her eyes and stretched.

"Bean, everything in my closet feels stale. If my jeans don't get a few new shirts to play with, they're going to die of boredom."

The dog licked her paws.

"How am I supposed to go to the mall today and not buy a single thing?"

Bean barked once.

"Nice try, Bean, but Halloween costumes don't count," Massie said. "I'm talking about something new and cute and envy-worthy. I don't want anyone to think I'm slipping ever again."

"Honey, we're leaving in three minutes," Kendra's voice announced over the intercom.

"'Kay, Mom, I'll be right down." Massie spoke into the box on her night table.

But she was still in her underwear.

Massie peeked out of her bedroom window, hoping to catch a glimpse of Claire struggling to find something non-repetitive to wear. But her lights were off. She was probably already waiting downstairs.

UGH!

Massie's phone rang three times before she found it underneath a crumpled blazer.

"Hey, Kristen, what's up?"

"Nuthin'." Kristen sounded bummed.

"What's wrong?" Massie held a gray DKNY T-shirt up to her face, then tossed it over her shoulder.

"I can't believe you're not coming shopping with us," Kristen said. "This is the last Saturday before Halloween, and if we all want to wear the same costumes—"

"Do you honestly *think* I *want* to go with Claire?" Massie asked. "Or that I would *ever* pick her over you guys? Puh-*lease!* Have we met? I'm making this sacrifice for the greater good of the party and you know it."

"Sorry. It's just that I'm kind of bummed about Dylan

liking Derrington, and Alicia is obviously taking her side because she says Dylan was talking about her crush way before I was, but that's only because I told *you* and not Alicia."

While Kristen talked, Massie tried to think of a way to be seen with her friends. What if they bumped into Becca or Liz? It wouldn't look good if she wasn't there.

"Hey, don't you guys have plans to go to the mall today?" Massie asked.

"No. We're going to—"

"Kristen, don't you guys have plans to go to the mall today?" Massie's words were razor sharp.

"Oh yeah, right," Kristen said. "We've been planning it for days."

"But remember, you have to act like it was a total accident," Massie said. "My mom thinks Claire and I are quote *friends* end quote. If she thinks I had anything to do with this, the party will be off."

"No problem. Acting is my specialty. My mom still thinks I wear old-lady cardigans and baggy slacks to school every day, doesn't she? We'll call you when we get there."

The girls hung up and Massie turned to face her closet one last time.

She decided the only way to survive the bet was to treat her old clothes in new ways. This way her mind would be tricked into thinking that she had gone shopping. She threaded one of her father's Armani ties (left over from her short-lived Avril phase) through the loops of her Sevens so it would swing across the outside of her leg when she walked. Then she slid a white Brooks Brothers shirt (mostly for sleeping) over her tank top. She left every button open except the bottom two. Once the sleeves were rolled up and her charm bracelet was fastened, she was ready.

"Boarding school chic," she said to Bean.

"We're leaving," Kendra said through the intercom.

Massie walked downstairs and greeted the mothers, Claire, and Todd with a smile. She was pleased to see Claire standing uncomfortably in an ultra-tight mustard yellow T-shirt that barely covered her midriff.

"How does it feel to have your sister borrow your clothes?" Massie asked Todd.

He was standing by the front door, eating a banana.

"Ha! I knew she would notice," Todd said to Claire with a cocky grin.

His voice was thick and garbled because he spoke with his mouth full. The gooey sound made Massie's stomach turn.

Claire scowled at her brother.

"It's laundry day, that's all," she said to Massie. "Besides, we never said anything about borrowing."

"Go for it. Seeing you in Todd's clothes is almost better than imagining you in my old snowsuit." Massie twisted the dangling tie around her wrist as she spoke.

"Don't get used to it," Claire said. "My mom told me I could buy a few new things at the mall today."

Massie couldn't believe how cruel life could be. The corners of her mouth felt like they were carving their way through drying cement as she forced a that's-so-great-I couldn't-be-happier-for-you-if-I-tried smile across her face.

"So you've been keeping track of my ensembles, have you?" Todd whispered all over the back of Massie's neck. "Did you happen to notice the new gray Dockers I got last week?"

His hot breath smelled like banana.

"Did you happen to notice my two-inch Choos?"

She lowered the heel of her boot on Todd's foot. He let out a soft yelp and limped over to his mother's side.

"Love hurts," Massie said.

THE WESTCHESTER MALL

LEVEL I

12:51 PM

October 25th

Claire and Todd ran through the automatic doors of The Westchester like they had just been dropped at Six Flags.

"Think they have a Dairy Queen here?" Todd shouted to Claire. He was trailing behind because of his recent foot injury.

"Every mall has a Dairy Queen," Claire yelled over her shoulder. "Massie, wanna come find the gummy store with me?"

"I'd rather not waste my calories," Massie said while checking her cell phone for messages.

Claire immediately thought of her friends back home. They all loved candy. They bought it together, shared it, and kept emergency supplies stashed away in their closets. The girls in Westchester acted the exact same way. Only to them "candy" equaled shoes and handbags, not sours.

Claire put her hand in the back pocket of her black satin dress pants (ugh, this stupid bet!) and ran her fingertips along the three dollar bills her father gave her before she left the house. She vowed to wean herself off sugar after this final indulgence. The Briarwood boys might think it was immature. Massie definitely did.

"Remember," Kendra announced. "We're meeting in front of Nordstrom's in ten minutes."

Sunshine poured through the skylights, filling the mall with warm light. The Westchester looked nothing like the concrete barns Claire and her friends shopped at in Florida. It didn't even have a Spencer Gifts or a Strawberry. Instead shoppers wove in and out of Louis Vuitton, Sephora, and Versace Jeans Couture. They wore big movie-star sunglasses and high heels that clicked and clacked on the shiny marble floors with every step they took.

Claire felt like the stylish mannequins in the window displays were looking down on her, just like Massie, Alicia, Kristen, and Dylan did.

Claire didn't feel comfortable until she set foot in the Sweet Factory. Familiar bins of colorful candy lined the walls and felt like home. She scooped a mound of gummies into a plastic bag and paid the cashier.

"Thank you for visiting the Sweet Factory." The overweight teenager managed to hand Claire her change without looking up from his copy of *Dr. Atkins' New Diet Revolution.*

"No," Claire said. "Thank *you.*" She popped an orange gummy foot in her mouth and headed back to meet the others.

Massie was the last to arrive at Nordstrom's and the only one who wasn't chomping on a sugary snack. Even Judi and Kendra were sharing a big black-and-white cookie.

"It must be hard to be around all of these stores and not shop, huh?" Claire said to Massie.

"I don't know," Massie said. "I haven't really thought about it."

But Claire knew Massie was lying by the way she stared

longingly at people's bags when they passed. Suddenly Claire hated herself for suggesting the bet in the first place. Her goal was to be accepted by Massie, not resented.

"Want some calories?" Todd said to Massie. He held out a sticky Cinnabon.

"No thanks."

"C'mon, just a bite. Taste the *sin* in Cinnabon."

"No THANKS."

"It's ha-ah-t." Todd waved the pastry under her nose.

"Todd, did I order coffee?" Massie said.

"Uh, no," Todd answered.

"Then why are you all up in my MUG?" Massie snapped.

"S'cuse me for offering," Todd said. He backed away.

Claire giggled. She was digging through a bag of gummies, trying to avoid the green ones.

"Want some of these?" Claire offered the bag to Massie even though she knew it was a waste of time.

Massie reached in and pulled out a handful. Todd's jaw dropped.

"Oh, sure, you'll eat with *Claire,*" he said. "Since when did you start liking *her* more than me?"

"Since always," Massie said.

Todd was so hurt he ran ahead to catch up with the mothers. Claire, on the other hand, was elated. Massie actually liked *her* better than someone. So what if it was her bratty brother? It was a start.

"He won't be bothering you for at least another hour," Claire said.

Massie responded by grabbing more gummies.

The two girls slowed their pace to let Todd and the mothers get ahead of them.

"So what are you going to be for Halloween?" Claire asked.

"A Dirty Devil," Massie said. It came out sounding like "a Duree Devuh" because she was chewing on a gummy worm. "You?"

"I was thinking maybe Blossom, the Powerpuff Girl. She's got brains, beauty, and a mean punch. And I already have the costume from last year."

"That's all right, I guess. At least you're not one of those people who goes for the punny costumes," Massie said. "You know, like a black-eyed *p* or a card shark."

"Yeah, those costumes are so wanna-be clever." Claire had never really given "punny costumes" much thought before but decided to agree anyway.

"I think you two should wear the same costumes since you're co-hosts," Kendra called out over her shoulder.

"How did she hear us?" Claire mouthed to Massie.

"What a cute idea," Judi chimed in.

Massie touched Claire's arm lightly as if to say, "Stand back and let me deal with this one."

"Mom, that's a great idea if only we thought of it a few days ago," Massie said. "It's just that I already have a costume commitment with Alicia, Dylan, and Kristen. Oh, and Claire *really* wants to be a Powerpuff Girl, so maybe next year."

"Oh, come on. You could go as the PARTYpuff Girls," Judi said.

Claire rolled her eyes. She thought she'd die of embarrassment.

"Uh, that's okay," Massie said. "Things are fine the way they are."

"Claire, wouldn't you rather be a Dirty Devil with Massie and her friends?" Kendra asked.

"Uh, yeah, I guess, but—"

"You were a Powerpuff Girl last year," Judi said.

"I know, but—"

Claire could feel Massie glaring at her.

"Then it's settled." Kendra pulled something invisible from her long eyelashes. "You'll both be Dirty Devils."

Claire's stomach dropped like she was going down a steep roller coaster.

"Uh, okay," she said.

Todd looked at Massie and giggled. He quickly brought his icing-covered hand to his mouth.

"Sorry," Claire muttered under her breath.

But Massie turned her head away and tugged on her Armani tie belt.

Claire stepped into her line of sight and tried to apologize again, but Massie crossed her arms and said nothing.

Claire had the chilling suspicion that Massie would start acting like a devil a few days earlier than planned.

The Westchester Mall
Level II
1:38 PM
October 25th

Massie couldn't believe she was standing in The Limited. The store's cheap knockoffs had always been an endless source of jokes among her friends. Alicia called their fake wannabe Prada bags Fraudas, and Dylan referred to their tweed page boy caps as "craps." But at that moment, Massie would have given anything for one of their shiny BO-inducing polyester sweaters like the one Claire was trying on.

Massie grabbed a pair of red fishnet hose off the rack near the cash register. The Dirty Devil costume originally called for bare legs, but she was drawn to the "bad girl" quality of the fishnets. Or was she? She put them back on the rack and decided to stick to the original plan. *But maybe the fishnets are better.* She picked them up again. But instead of looking at the tights, she focused on Claire, who ran from rack to rack, deciding what to buy next.

"Claire," Massie snapped. She stuffed the hose back on the rack. "It's hard for me to concentrate on our costumes with you bolting all over the store, trying to buy tacky sweaters."

"Sorry," Claire said. "There's nothing I like here anyway." She tiptoed away from Massie, the excitement on her face fading.

Massie walked aimlessly around the store, touching fabrics

and forcing herself to walk past the colorful stacks of camisoles and cardigans. She was about to cave and try on the only thing with cute potential in the entire store (a navy-and-pink fuzzy scarf) when she received the text message she had been waiting for.

KRISTEN: ? R U?
MASSIE: THE LIMITED. HELP!
KRISTEN: STAY CALM. WE'RE COMING.
MASSIE: ACT NATCH.
KRISTEN: GIVEN.

Seconds later Kristen, Alicia, and Dylan appeared in The Limited.

"Oh my God, is that Massie?" Alicia shouted across the store.

Massie tossed her last gummy worm in the round clothes rack as soon as she heard them.

"I—I think it is," Dylan said. "Hey, Mass. What on earth are you *doing* here?"

Dylan waved frantically from the other side of the store.

"Now, isn't that a coincidence," Kendra said to Massie. "You must be so surprised."

"I am." Massie put her hand on her heart for effect and went to greet her friends.

Their arms were full of shiny, tissue-stuffed shopping bags from Versace Jeans, Sephora, and BCBG.

"You didn't see Becca or anyone while you were shopping without me, did you?" Massie whispered.

They shook their heads.

"Good," Massie said quietly.

"What are you guys doing here?" Massie's voice was now loud and clear.

"You mean us?" Dylan shouted. "Oh, we had this day planned for months."

Massie shot her a look. "You call that acting? You did a better job playing a flying monkey in *The Wizard of Oz* when we were seven."

"I told you to be subtle," Kristen said. "You were waving like you were about to set sail on the *Titanic.*"

Massie could feel her mother's eyes burning a hole in her back.

"Go to the dressing rooms and I'll sneak in as soon as I can," Massie said.

"Cute tie belt thing, by the way," Alicia said.

"Thanks," Massie said. She meant it. That compliment had been the only good part of her day.

She watched her friends as they tried to squeeze their bags past the mannequins and displays on their way to the back of the store.

"Massie," Kendra said quickly. She said it the same way she said "Bean" when the dog picked through the trash.

"Uh-huh?" Massie smiled innocently but kept her distance.

Kendra signaled for her to come closer.

"I have the feeling that you and Claire aren't getting along as well as you were the other night," she said. "Is everything okay?"

"Of course. Why?"

"Well, I thought you two wanted to spend the day together, and now I see your friends are here." Kendra checked to make sure they were alone by the hair accessories display.

"The truth is, dear," she said softly, "Judi is concerned. She doesn't think Claire has hit her social stride yet and really wants you both to get along."

"Everything is *fine,*" Massie said. "Don't worry, okay?" She started to back away, but her mother grabbed her thin wrist and stopped her.

"I hope so, because Judi and Claire are two of the sweetest people I know, and I would hate to see them upset."

"Mom, everything is—"

"She would be devastated if she thought you were lying about your friendship with Claire just to get permission for your party. It would also mean calling the whole thing off, and I know how much everyone in your grade has been looking forward to it."

"You have nothing to worry about, okay?" Massie stood on her tiptoes and kissed her mother on the cheek. "I was just on my way to find Claire before you stopped me. So can I *please* go help her shop? She needs me."

"Yes," Kendra sighed. "You may want to suggest she try black. It will look so pretty with her bright eyes."

Massie gave her mother the thumbs-up sign and hurried off. But Claire was the last thing on her mind.

THE LIMITED
DRESSING ROOM NO. 5
2:12 PM
October 25th

"I have about two minutes before my mother gets suspicious, so I'll make this quick," Massie whispered. "Remember that bet I told you about? Well, it's killing me—I have nothing to wear."

"Why don't you just admit defeat?" Alicia said. "It's only a bet."

"Because then she has to wear her old snowsuit to school for a week," Kristen said.

"It's two weeks," Dylan said.

"No, it isn't, it's one week," Kristen said.

"Ehmagod, will you guys please stop fighting already? I need your help."

Massie reached into her red Coach clutch and pulled out her Visa.

"Take this and buy me some cute tops. I would love a purple scoop neck and maybe something in winter white and then whatever else you think I'll like. I'll take care of our costumes if you do this for me."

"Don't forget I lost five pounds, so I probably went down a size," Dylan said.

"Got it," Massie barked. "Now go!"

The girls stormed out, eager to complete their mission.

Massie breathed a sigh of relief. She fixed her hair, reapplied her lip gloss, and adjusted her tie belt before unlocking the dressing room door. She had just saved her dying wardrobe, and she felt at peace for the first time all day. Her next stop would be The Espresso Bar for a celebratory chai latte.

Massie was greeted by a mob of impatient shoppers holding armfuls of clothes, waiting for her to leave. But her victory was too sweet to be soured by a bunch of Limited customers, and besides, it wasn't like she'd ever see *them* again.

She held her head high and walked out of the dressing room, managing to avoid eye contact with everyone.

"I heard you."

Massie knew the voice but kept going.

"I know what you're doing."

Don't look back. Left foot, right foot. Left foot, right foot. Keep moving. You're almost out!

"Massie, STOP," Claire said. She was at the front of the line, holding a periwinkle blue sweater and a few other items from the sale rack.

"What did you hear?" Massie said.

"I don't want to fight." Claire's voice was patient and kind. "I know this has been hard for you, so I'll give you another chance. You can either call your friends to tell them you've changed your mind. Or you can wear the new sweaters under your old snowsuit." Claire had an evil grin on her face. It gave Massie goose bumps.

Massie lifted her phone out of her bag and flipped it open.

"Darn," she said, and snapped it shut. "Battery's dead."

"Here you go," said a girl with dreadlocks who happened

to be in line behind Claire. She handed over her red-gold-and-green Nokia. "You're Massie Block, right? You go to OCD, right?"

Massie waved the phone away and accidentally inhaled a mouthful of patchouli.

"Yeah," she said. "Who are you?"

"Brianna Grossman."

"Are you new?" Massie asked.

"No, we've been in the same class for two years," Brianna said, looking confused. "You invited me to your Halloween party."

But Massie didn't respond. Instead she used her thumb to open her cell phone and her middle finger to flip Claire off.

THE BLOCK ESTATE
MASSIE'S BEDROOM
7:42 AM
October 31st

Massie had just stepped out of the shower and was dripping wet when her phone rang.

The caller was unidentified.

"Hello? Oh . . . uh . . . hi, Jocelyn . . . uh-huh . . . Well, why are you RSVP'ing to me?"

Massie wiped the steam off the mirror so she could watch herself talk on the phone. She looked annoyed. "You're supposed to call Kuh-laire . . . not *me.*"

Jocelyn stammered while she rushed to explain that Massie's name had been on her invite, not Claire's. But Massie wasn't paying attention. She was replacing the damp towel around her body with a fresh warm one off the heated rack. She was finished in the bathroom and done with Jocelyn.

"Do you hear that buzzing?" Massie asked.

"No."

"There must be something wrong with my phone," Massie said. "I can't hear—"

She hung up and tossed the phone onto her bed.

"Why did she call *me?*" Massie said to Bean as she towel-dried her hair.

When she flipped her head back up, she noticed the five Dirty Devil costumes splayed across her purple duvet. Inez must have finished working on them late last night and dropped them off while she was in the shower.

Red pleated microminis (which were once frumpy knee-length skirts), with long arrow-tipped tails sewed onto the back, lined the foot of the bed. Above each one was a pair of gray boy shorts with *Kiss It* written across the butt in silver glitter. Tiny black Petit Bateau tanks with strategically placed rips and tears were splayed out like a fan. Massie checked the top left side of each one, the spot usually reserved for the designer's logo, to make sure her instructions were properly executed. They were. Red stitching personalized each girl's costume—*Massie Devil, Kristen Devil, Alicia Devil, Dylan Devil,* and *Claire Devil.* Massie could barely look at the last one. It just didn't belong. Right beside Bean's doggie bed was a tiny black shirt that said *Bean Devil* across the back, but Massie was too upset to smile.

"Bean, you are the fifth, not *her,*" Massie said.

Bean blinked.

She heard a familiar honk and knew that Isaac, her driver, was ready to take her to school. Massie, still in her towel, searched for something exciting to wear.

In the last week she had done ties for belts, earrings pinned to blazers, dresses over jeans. She'd even mismatched her boots and worn one black and one brown. But now that it was Friday, she was tapped.

The fashionably challenged would look to her for weekend outfit ideas, and they deserved to see something fabulous.

If they didn't, they would find another style muse. And Massie couldn't let that happen.

The horn blasted one more time and Massie contemplated faking sick. She had to think fast. She quickly reached for her Halloween costume and slid it on, admiring the flattering fit. There was little left to the imagination, but, *Hey,* she thought, *it's Halloween.*

Massie grabbed Alicia, Kristen, and Dylan's costumes and bolted out the door. She was in such a hurry, she accidentally left Claire's behind.

At least that was what she'd tell her mother.

Octavian Country Day School
The Halls
8:25 AM
October 31st

The girls always turned heads when they walked the halls of OCD, but when the four Dirty Devils passed, students stood in awe.

They looked striking and confident in their matching costumes. Like a gang of sexy fembots on a mission to take over suburbia. Everyone who passed either complimented them on their daring outfits or told them how excited they were about the party.

"This is a huge mistake," Kristen muttered.

"Why?" Massie asked. She didn't look at Kristen when she spoke because that would ruin the blank runway model stare she was working for the crowd. It felt great to be wearing something new, and she didn't want Kristen's insecurities to ruin the moment.

"OCD has a pretty strict 'no skin' policy and we're breaking it on like five different counts," Kristen said. "According to the OCD manual, we're supposed to be covered from the top of our boobs to an inch above our knees and—"

"Puh-lease," Alicia chimed in. "It's Halloween. No one will care."

"Yeah and even if they do, so what?" Dylan added. "The

last skimpy outfit I was thin enough to fit into was designed by Pampers."

By third period there had been at least four Dirty Devil wanna-be sightings. By lunch there were eight.

"There's another one," Alicia said, pointing to Jaedra Russell.

She was ahead of them in line at the Café, wearing a super-short jean skirt and a black V-neck that had been torn just below the ribs.

"We've started more trends in one day than Marc Jacobs has in a year," Kristen said.

They slid their trays a few inches closer to the cash register.

"Aren't you so glad to be one of us?" Massie said to her friends, then answered her ringing cell phone.

"Speaking," she said with an eye roll. "It's AUDREY," she mouthed.

"You'll be at the party tonight? . . . Well, I'd be excited too if I was you . . . *really* excited, considering you've never been invited to one of my parties before." Massie covered the mouthpiece so she could join her friends, who were hysterically laughing. "How did you get my number? . . . Really. Are you sure it didn't say Claire? You never were a good reader. . . ."

Dylan grabbed the cell phone away from Massie's ear and pressed end. The girls cracked up. Audrey called back, but this time Massie hit ignore and dropped the phone in her Prada messenger bag.

"That's the fifth call I've gotten this week from an LBR,"

Massie said. "And unfortunately every one of them has RSVP'd 'yes.'"

"Is Derrington coming?" Dylan asked as she pulled the loose skirt up over her hips.

"Yup, and so are all of his cute friends," Massie said.

Trays in hand, the four girls made their way through the sea of lunch tables, stopping every so often to chat with their adoring fans about the highly anticipated boy-girl party that was only hours away.

"Massie, is it true that Landon Dorsey is doing your party?" Mandy Ross asked.

"Totally," Massie said. "She said this party is going to be one of her best."

"Will there be sugar-free candy?" Suze Gayner asked.

"If Dylan's Candy Bar makes it, we'll have it," Massie said.

"Are you guys wearing the Dirty Devil costumes tonight or do you have something else planned?" Vanessa Covers asked.

"You'll have to wait and find out." Kristen shook her glittery butt.

"Can I bring a dance mix I burned last night?" Ava Waters said.

"Totally."

"Is it true that Becca Wilder thought of the boy-girl party first?" Parker Lemons asked.

"What do *you* think?" Massie looked Parker straight in the eye. The girl responded with a nervous giggle.

"We should have held a press conference," Massie said when she sat down.

"Seriously," Dylan said. "Can you believe Allyson asked if your house had any good make-out spots?"

"I know," Kristen said. "Hopefully the only thing going on her lips tonight is a tube of ChapStick. Did you see all those cracks?"

"Any more calls from your new BFFs, aka the LBRs?" Alicia asked Massie.

"Jocelyn was telling everyone in math that she spoke to you this morning before school," Kristen said.

"No way!" Massie said.

"I swear. Then two seconds later Liza and Hope said *they* spoke to you last night," Dylan said. "I think Hope even said you guys talked for hours."

"NO WAY!"

"I heard that too," Kristen said.

"Ehmagod, that *can't* be good for your reputation." Alicia twisted open her bottle of Perrier and the whole thing fizzed over and soaked her California rolls.

"Great, thanks a lot," Alicia said to a stranger at the table behind her.

"How is that my fault?" the girl said.

Alicia didn't respond.

"Did you tell everyone Hope was lying?" Massie asked Dylan.

"I was about to, but the teacher walked in."

Massie's head started to spin. The sound of everyone talking in the Café suddenly seemed too loud to bear and the dirt smell of the grilling veggie burgers made her want to puke.

She took a deep breath and let it out slowly. She waited for the panic to pass before she spoke.

"If Hope and the other LBRs are saying I've been talking to them on the phone, people might think I *like* them. I'll be ruined."

"That *is* brutal," Kristen said. "How did they get your number?"

Massie had a hunch but was interrupted before she could answer.

"Can I talk to you for a minute?" Claire asked. She was wearing a faded Good Charlotte concert tee and a loose patchy jean skirt. Both were obviously borrowed from Layne.

"Go ahead," Massie said.

"I mean in private," Claire said.

"She's gonna tell us everything you say, so you might as well just talk to her here," Dylan said.

"Fine." Claire pushed her bangs to the side of her forehead and tried to tuck them behind her ear, but they weren't quite long enough to make it. "I thought we were going to wear the same costumes tonight."

"We are." Massie's voice was flat and impatient.

"Yeah, but now I can't wear mine because all the boys will think I went home after school and copied you," Claire explained.

"Believe me, none of the boys will be giving you or your costume a second thought tonight," Massie said. "Besides, how are they going to know what we wore to school today?"

"Supposedly everyone at Briarwood has already heard

about your sexy costumes," Claire said. "The boys have been talking about them all day."

"Really?" Massie's face lit up. She forgot all about the Losers Beyond Repair for a second.

"Why didn't you tell me you were going to wear your costumes today?" Claire asked. Her voice trembled. "I could have worn mine too."

Massie stood up and placed her hands on her hips.

"Normally I would make up an excuse so I wouldn't have to tell you straight to your face that I never wanted you to be a part of our costumes. But since you decided to put my cell phone number on every loser's invitation in the greater New York area, I'm not going to bother," Massie said. "Who cares what our mothers say at this point? The party is a done deal. Go be Elmo or whatever it was you were going to be and leave me alone."

Claire opened her mouth like she was about to say something big, but before anything came out, she took off. Massie saw Layne get up from her seat by the bathrooms and chase after her. Massie secretly hoped Claire wouldn't tell on her, but she was too mad at the moment to try and stop her.

"To the Dirty Devils," Massie said, raising her glass of lemon water.

"To the Dirty Devils," they all repeated back.

Octavian Country Day School
Nurse Adele's Office
8:42 AM
October 31st

Claire burst through the door of Nurse Adele's office. She turned to her whenever she needed a sympathetic ear at school.

"Claire, is someone after you?" Adele asked.

Claire wanted to laugh, but she was too distraught.

"You know how you told me to stand up to Massie?" Claire said. "Well, I did."

"And?" Adele said.

"Let's just say she was taller," Claire said.

"What happened?" Adele asked.

"It's nothing. Just a little confusion over a costume. I really just came to say hi and wish you a happy Halloween." Claire knew she had started this fight with Massie by giving her phone number to the LBRs, but she was too ashamed to admit it to Adele.

Claire took a handful of candy corn from the glass dish on Adele's desk and dropped them into her mouth. The taste reminded her of her friends back home in Orlando, and she wondered what they would be dressing up as this year.

"I thought I'd find you here," Layne said as she entered the office. "Are you okay? I could tell by the way you bolted out of the Café that things didn't go so well with Massie.

Did you ask Adele if you could look through the rack of clothes in the lost and found? You know, maybe you can actually go as 'lost 'n' found' or something."

"Do you still need a costume, Claire?" Adele asked. "Because you're more than welcome to take—"

"No, that's okay." Claire didn't want Adele to think the only reason she came to visit was to look for clothes. "I still have the Powerpuff Girls costume I wore last year. I'll just be Blossom again."

Claire hated the way Layne was looking at her. Tilted head, wide eyes, crossed arms, and a do-you-want-to-talk-about-the-pain look on her face. Claire knew her friend was only trying to help, but she needed to get her confidence back, and a good cry wasn't part of that process. A few minutes alone in her bedroom with a mirror and a few nobody-can-bring-me-down songs and she'd be better than ever. Now if only Layne would stop staring at her. . . .

The next girl to throw open the door was Amber Ryan. She was hunched over and holding her side as if she'd just crawled off the front lines of a battlefield.

"Nurse!" she cried. "Call 411."

"Why? Do you need a local listing?" Layne asked.

Claire covered her mouth in a desperate attempt not to crack up.

"Amber, do you mind if I take a look?" Adele said.

Amber shook her head, then wiped her tears away with the back of her hand. She lifted the side of her sweater slowly, bracing the nurse for a hideous sight.

Claire and Layne leaned down to peek at the wound just when Adele did and they all bumped heads. Claire burst out laughing, which made Amber start to cry all over again.

"Shhh, it's okay," Adele said. "It's only a scrape. A little disinfectant and you'll be just fine."

Amber's sobs were reduced to light tears, which gradually became sniffles.

"What happened?" Adele asked.

"I tried to cut my sweater with scissors and I slipped," Amber said, as if that was as common as dropping her books on the way to class. She must have noticed Nurse Adele's puzzled look, because she continued explaining without even being asked.

"Massie and her friends came to school today in these really amazing super-skimpy ripped tops and everyone's been trying to do the same thing to their clothes," Amber said. "I feel like such an idiot."

"For trying to follow them?" Layne said. "Well, you should."

"No, for cutting myself," Amber said. "Shari, Mel, Trina, and Shannyn cut their shirts, no problem."

Nurse Adele frowned.

"You mean other girls are doing this?"

"Everyone is," Amber said. "You would too if you saw how good it looked."

Claire could tell Adele was fuming because her nostrils were flared. She didn't even offer Amber a giant Hershey's

Kiss from the Feel Better Closet when she was done. Instead she stormed out of her office.

"Where are you going?" Claire shouted after her.

"To speak to Principal Burns," Adele called back. She marched down the hall toward the administrative offices. "This is a school. NOT a runway."

"Looks like Massie's in for a pretty scary Halloween," Layne said with a smile.

"I love this holiday." Claire reached for one more handful of candy corn before heading off to her next class.

OCTAVIAN COUNTRY DAY SCHOOL
PRINCIPAL BURNS'S OFFICE
1:27 PM
October 31st

"I told you we'd get in trouble," Kristen whispered to her friends. She was holding her stomach and rocking back and forth as if she had food poisoning. "My mother is never going to let me leave the house again. I'm going to be homeschooled."

They were all seated on The Bench, an antique church pew that was pressed up against the wall outside Principal Burns's office. They could just barely hear her clipped tones as she called their parents, one by one, to tell them about the "incident."

"This is so stupid," Massie said. "My parents raise so much money for this school and *this* is how they treat us? *Puh-lease!*"

"Don't worry." Dylan hooked a red curl with her pinky finger and tossed it away from her face. "I'll have my mom dedicate a whole episode of *The Daily Grind* to this injustice." Whenever Dylan didn't approve of a situation, she threatened to have her famous mother expose it on her hit morning show. "She hates when people try to force their beliefs on others, especially when it involves the arts."

"Enough talking, girls, this is an office, not a birthday party." The cranky secretary whipped off her tortoiseshell glasses and twirled them around her index finger. When she finished glaring at the girls, she slid the glasses back on her head and returned to her computer.

"She thinks she's in the Wild, Wild Westchester," Massie whispered.

The girls giggled.

"One more sound and I'll blast the air-conditioning," the secretary said. "Your half-naked bodies will be frozen solid in under ten seconds."

Massie slowly opened her phone and the other girls did the same, except for Kristen. She was too busy twisting long pieces of blond hair around her shaking fingers.

MASSIE: LOOK AT THE DOOR.
DYLAN: WHAT?
MASSIE: THE SIGN. READ IT.
ALICIA: P. BURNS. SO?
MASSIE: SO C A DR.

All three girls burst out laughing, which made Kristen turn purple with rage.

"If she hears you laugh, she'll get even madder," she said, pointing to the principal's office.

"What's she going to do?" Massie asked. "Dress us to death?"

"Precisely, Ms. Block," Principal Burns said.

Massie's jaw dropped when she saw the tall, scrawny, gray-haired woman standing above her. Rumor had it that Principal Burns picked orange peels out of the garbage can and ate them because they were packed with antioxidants. To keep from getting scared, Massie tried to picture her digging through the trash. It wasn't working.

"Each of your parents has been notified, and they will deal with you however they see fit," she continued. "But as long as you are in *my* school, you are to dress like young ladies, NOT Vegas showgirls." She lifted her watch right up to her eyeballs and checked the time. "Please report to Nurse Adele's office immediately and cover yourselves up with the garments she keeps in the lost and found. If I see so much as a fingernail uncovered, I'll have you all arrested for indecent exposure. Now go!"

The girls left in silence and did what they were told. Unfortunately, Claire had taken anything remotely decent over the last few weeks, so there wasn't a lot to choose from. After sifting through last season's rejects Massie, Kristen, Dylan, and Alicia emerged in time for fifth period. They still turned heads when they walked down the hall, but this time it was for all the wrong reasons.

Massie wore a bright red T-shirt that had a chocolate stain right above her left boob, which unfortunately matched the pair of XXL mustard-colored cords that she had to hold up when she walked.

Alicia found a floor-length denim skirt and paired it with a Gap jean shirt. Alicia called it a "rodeo-chic" look, but Massie simply referred to it as "rodee-oh no, you didn't!"

Dylan was forced to squeeze into a pair of Sevens that she had to leave unbuttoned because they were too small.

She matched them with a long tie-dyed T-shirt that covered up the open fly.

Kristen was the only one who got to wear decent clothes—she changed back into the leave-the-house outfit she had stuffed in her locker earlier that morning.

"Having strict parents finally paid off," she said to herself as she buttoned up the itchy tweed blazer her mother had bought her at Macy's.

On their way to class they passed two girls wearing torn T-shirts and miniskirts.

"Those ripped shirts are sooo out," Massie hissed as she passed them.

"Already?" one of the girls asked.

"Try to keep up, will ya?" Massie walked past them, knowing they were memorizing her outfit, trying to get a handle on the latest trend.

She couldn't wait for Monday, when half the girls in her grade would be dressed like Winnie-the-Pooh.

The Block Estate

The Guesthouse

6:05 PM

October 31st

Claire watched from her bedroom window as Landon Dorsey and her team of loyal manservants ran around the backyard, making sure every last corpse was in place. The house was filled with the sweet smell of her mother's caramel apples, but not even *that* could calm her down. The party was less than an hour away and Claire was still in her school clothes. Knowing that her brother and his incredibly tiny friend Nathan were behind closed doors putting the finishing touches on their Halloween costumes stressed her out even more.

Claire went over to her closet and pulled out a box marked Holiday Clothes. She opened the cardboard flaps and stuck her arm inside to search for last year's Powerpuff Girls costume.

How am I going to explain to my mother why I'm not dressed like my charming co-host?

Her fingers brushed against a smooth satin-polyester blend and she breathed a sigh of relief.

Found it!

"Claire, can we come in?" Todd called through her bedroom door. "We want to show you something."

"Can't it wait? I'm about to get dressed," Claire shouted back.

"No." Todd walked into her room.

"What are you *doing?*" Claire asked.

He was dressed as Bubbles and Nathan was dressed as Buttercup, the other two Powerpuff Girls. Nathan wore a mint green minidress with a thick black sash around the middle and a short black wig. Todd's dress was the same, only blue. Claire wondered how he had managed to divide his blond wig into two perfect pigtails but was too stunned to ask. Huge cardboard cutout eyes were taped to their sunglasses.

"I figured you'd probably feel like a gigantic loser going as Blossom if you had no one else to play the other Puffs," Todd said. "So we decided to help you out."

"That's not what you told *me,*" Nathan said to Todd. "You said no will know who we are in these costumes so we'll be able to mess with Massie and her hot friends."

"What are you *talking* about, Nathan?" Todd said, trying his hardest to sound confused.

"Anyway, Mom wants us downstairs for pictures in ten. So hurry up, Blossom." Todd gave Claire an energetic two-thumbs-up. "And remember, Powerpuffs save the day!"

Claire whipped a fuzzy pink slipper at him and hit a black-and-white photo of Massie's grandfather instead. It crashed to the ground but didn't break.

"Get out!"

Todd and Nathan raced out, screaming and laughing. They slammed the door shut behind them.

Claire heard the muffled sound of "Monster Mash" coming

from the DJ booth, and the pre-party jitters kicked in. She suddenly felt like she had to go to the bathroom.

"Claire," Judi shouted from the kitchen.

Claire didn't answer. She was too focused on zipping up her pink dress and adjusting her red wig.

"Claire," Judi yelled again.

"WHAT?"

Claire was tired of the constant interruptions. All she wanted was five minutes to get ready and give herself a pep talk in front of the mirror before the party started. She needed to work on her confidence if she was going to look for a boyfriend.

"Come on," Jay said. "It's picture time. The party's about to start."

"COMING."

Claire put on her mask and made her way downstairs even though she didn't feel completely ready to face her public.

"Oh, how cute!" Judi said when she saw Claire.

"You decided to dress up like your brother and Nathan," her father said.

"What?" Claire shot her brother a look. "It was *my*—" But she stopped, suddenly remembering that her mother expected her to be a Dirty Devil.

Claire didn't know what to say next. If she told her mother what happened at school, Massie would get in trouble. And the thought of Massie's wrath made the insides of Claire's stomach bunch up in fear. She would hunt Claire down like a limited edition Motorola and destroy her like last year's Ugg boots. Claire's appetite for Halloween candy was completely gone.

"Yeah," Todd said interrupting her. He widened his eyes just enough for Claire to notice. This usually meant she should shut up and follow his lead, but she couldn't imagine where he was taking her.

"Mom, I know you wanted her to dress up like Massie, but me and Nate really needed a third, so we begged her and she finally said yes. You're not mad, are you?"

Claire shrugged and gave a what-can-you-do? look.

"How could I be mad at that?" Judi smiled lovingly. "I think it's incredibly thoughtful."

"Okay," Jay said as he took the lens cap off his camera. "Picture time."

Jay started snapping and Judi directed the kids, suggesting different poses so their pictures would have variety.

"How did you know about my costume with Massie?" Claire asked Todd through her fake smile.

"I happened to overhear your phone conversation with Layne," Todd said through his teeth.

"Why did you lie for me?" Claire whispered.

"Sometimes I like to use my powers for good instead of evil. And I figured you could repay me by doing my math homework this weekend," he said.

"Fine," Claire said.

It was either that or admit to her parents that their dream—to have her and Massie become friends—would never be more than a fantasy.

The Block Estate
Massie's Bedroom

6:50 PM

October 31st

Massie was standing in front of her full-length mirror, trying to slide the devil horns onto her head without ruining her perfect part. It would have been easier if she wasn't talking on her cell phone at the same time, but she was late.

"Kristen, try to stop crying," Massie said. "I can't understand what you're saying."

"My" (gasp) "Mom" (sniff) "won't let me" (sharp inhale) "go tonight." Kristen let out a final sob.

"Tell her it's an all-girls party."

"It's not that." Kristen blew her nose into the phone. "It's the call she got from Principal Burns about our outfits today. I knew we should never have worn—"

"No offense, but your mother's way too strict." Massie straightened the devil's tail on the back of her skirt. "When I got home, my dad gave me a two-second speech about obeying school rules and went right back to downloading an audio book off the Internet."

"You're so lucky you have cool parents," Kristen said.

"Can't you just sneak out?" Massie asked.

"No way! I'm already in enough trouble."

"Well, it will totally suck if Dylan steals Derrington."

Kristen started crying even harder.

Massie knew that comment was the last thing Kristen wanted to hear as soon as she said it, but she was upset that her friend was going to miss her party. Massie wished that just this once, Kristen would stand up to her parents.

"Kidding," Massie said. "I'm sure she won't even have the guts to talk to him."

"Yeah, right." Kristen sniffed. "Ever since she lost weight, she's been a total flirt."

"Don't worry. I'll call you, 'kay?" Massie knew she should have been more comforting, but she had five minutes to get Bean in her Dirty Devil outfit, and her makeup wasn't even close to finished.

After fifteen more minutes of primping, Massie was finally ready. By seven o'clock she was in position by the side gate, ready to greet her guests. It was a warm night, especially for October, which made the backyard feel as magical as it looked.

"Everyone is going to be talking about this for the next fifty years," Landon said as she zipped by carrying a venti cup of coffee and a box filled with skull candles.

Massie's heart was so full of pride, she thought she was going to burst.

A huge banner hung above the entrance that said, WHEN HELL FREEZES OVER. It was written in red paint that looked like dripping blood. Waiters in red unitards dressed as Satan's helpers handed out orange-and-black tote bags so guests would have somewhere cute to keep their candy. A huge skating rink with a layer of mangled heads frozen below the surface had been placed beside the swimming pool. Two ghouls were stationed in one of the cabanas that had been converted into a booth full of rental skates. And mannequins hung off the massive oak tree dangling above the pool, which had been dyed red.

Three raging bonfires crackled and roared, casting an orange glow across the entire lawn. These "Pits of Despair" were surrounded by red blankets so the guests could sit on the ground and roast marshmallows with the wooden pitchforks that were laid out beside them.

The DJ was already playing music, Jules the caricature artist was setting up his easel, and the dry ice machine was casting an eerie fog that hovered above the top of the grass. Everything was in place except for one last detail.

Massie scribbled OUT OF ORDER on a piece of paper and stuck it to the door of one of the bathrooms by the pool. After all, every hostess needed a private place to rendezvous with her friends.

The first guests had started to arrive. Just as Massie had hoped, everyone was speechless when they walked through the gates.

"Massie, I think I've died and gone to hell!" Sadie Meltzer said, trying to be funny. She and her other B-list friends were dressed as princesses. Sadie always looked for an excuse to let her butt-length hair out of its ponytail, something her mother only agreed to on special occasions.

"This is the coolest party I've ever been to. You and Claire are amazing."

"Actually, Claire didn't have anything to do with it," Massie said. "Unless of course you count writing out the invitations."

Sadie said something back, but Massie could barely hear it. The only thing on her radar was Cam Fisher. He was approaching with Derrington and an unidentified person in a gorilla costume.

Massie thought the best thing about Cam was his eyes. One was green and one was blue. Alicia described his look as "psychotic husky," but Massie preferred "intense." Even though she was tempted, she stood by her decision not to tell anyone about her feelings until she was absolutely one hundred and ten percent sure that he liked her back. She had learned a lot from the humiliating mistake she'd made with Chris Abeley.

For weeks Massie had stalked him at Galwaugh Farms so they could ride their horses together. She ditched her friends to spend time with him and even pretended she was BFFs with his sister, Layne. All the while Massie had no idea that Chris only liked her as a friend; he was dating a disgustingly beautiful ninth grader named Fawn.

"Don't you look *vicious.*" Cam grimaced as he greeted Massie. She searched her brain for something clever to say about his costume, but he was dressed as a soccer goalie, so there wasn't much to work off of.

"What are *you* supposed to be?" she asked Derrington, hoping the abrupt subject change didn't tip them off to how nervous she was.

"A dirtbag," Derrington mumbled. His head was poking through the top of a green garbage bag that was smeared with mud. "So are these the famous costumes we heard about all over school today?" Derrington looked Massie up and down, but she wished Cam had noticed her instead. He was too busy pulling a twig out of the gorilla's facial fur.

Massie was getting ready to brag about how much trouble they got into at school when she was interrupted by a Powerpuff Girl.

"Hey, sorry I'm late. My parents made me pose for a thousand pictures before they'd let me leave the house." She turned to Derrington. "Hi, I'm Claire."

"You must be the new girl we've been hearing about," he said. Cam turned away from the gorilla to steal a look at her.

"You've *heard* of me?" Claire asked. But Massie pulled Claire away before they had a chance to answer.

"Look," she hissed. "There's no point in both of us standing in the same spot. Why don't you hang by the DJ booth in case people want to request a song or something? I'll stay here by the front and take care of the welcome thing."

Massie was relieved beyond belief when Claire left without putting up a fight. Now that *she* was out of the way,

Massie was free to focus on Cam. He was heading toward the treats table, and Massie tried to look casual by chatting and mingling while she followed closely behind. She was suddenly overcome by a strong craving for sugar.

CURRENT STATE OF THE UNION

IN	OUT
Dylan and Derrington	Kristen and Derrington
Massie and Cam Fisher	Massie and Chris Abeley
The "old Block"	The "new girl"

The Block Estate
When Hell Freezes Over Party

7:40 PM

October 31st

Claire made her way past the moaning zombie waitresses who were offering up "horror d'oeuvres." She got the hint that Massie wanted her to disappear, but she certainly wasn't going to spend the night standing beside the DJ booth. This was her party too.

"Hey, Blossom."

Claire turned to see Layne lumbering toward her. People cleared the way to let her pass, not so much because they were polite, but because they were scared they'd get knocked to the ground if they didn't.

"Wow, you really went for the whole couch potato thing, didn't you?" Claire said to her friend before snapping her picture. Layne was stuffed inside a horizontal refrigerator box. The pea green cushions from her basement sofa lined the top and her face was painted brown, like a potato.

"I love this holiday," Layne sighed.

Just then Alicia and Dylan walked by, twirling their tails and strutting their stuff.

"Oh, look, a couch poo," Alicia said to Dylan.

"I'm a couch POTATO." Layne adjusted her pillows. She looked at Claire and rolled her eyes.

"I'm glad you told me," Alicia said. "I was about to compliment you on your new dress."

"Yeah," Dylan said. "Anything's better than those janitor-friendly man pants you've been wearing lately."

"At least I *wore* a costume. You look the same as you always do," Layne said. "Identical to Massie."

Claire was so impressed by Layne's courage and quick wit she wanted to throw her arms around her friend and give her a hug. But that would have to wait until the box was gone.

"Yeah? Well, you look the same as *you* always do," Dylan said. "Stupid!"

Claire and Layne knew their comeback was much better and hurried over to greet their friends before a major fight broke out.

They made a few laps around the yard with Meena and Heather, who were dressed as dead versions of Paris and Nicky Hilton. They both wore blond wigs, barely there dresses, and green face paint. It looked like all seventy-five people showed up, and Claire couldn't help wondering if anyone would have come had it just been her name on the invitation.

For the most part, the boys were lingering around the treats table and the girls were hovering around the edges of the dance floor. Everyone seemed to be laughing and having a good time, but no one was mingling.

"This DJ is so Wal-Mart," Meena said. "When is he going to stop playing those cheesy Halloween songs and start playing something cool?"

"Now," Claire said. She led the way to the DJ booth.

"Excuse me." Claire used her most polite voice. "Hi. Um, do you think you could start playing some real songs soon?"

The DJ looked down at Claire from his booth and smiled so big the bottom of his goatee spread across his chin.

"I thought you'd never ask," he said. "That Landon Dorsey chick forced me to play this crap."

Seconds later Britney Spears's "Toxic" was blasting out of the speakers and everyone rushed the dance floor. Meena and Heather were the first ones out there. "It's what the Hilton sisters would have wanted," Heather said before they took off.

"Do you think anyone will ask me to dance in this stupid Powerpuff Girls costume?" Claire asked as she bobbed her head to the beat.

"See!" Layne shot her finger straight into the air like she had just made a brilliant discovery. "That's exactly why I didn't want you to invite the boys. If it was a girls-only party, you wouldn't care *how* you looked in your costume. You'd be dancing already."

"Yeah, and if it was girls only, I wouldn't have come," Claire said. "I've seen what these girls do for fun around here and it usually involves torturing *me.* So, if you won't introduce me to any boys, I'll do it myself."

"Oh, right." Layne smiled, amused, as if Claire had just told her she was swearing off gummies. "Better yet, why don't you ask your co-host to introduce you? I dare you."

Claire bit her lower lip.

"If I do, will you promise to stay and talk to the boys with me?"

"Totally," Layne said. She obviously didn't believe Claire would go through with it.

"Fine," Claire said. "I guess I have nothing to lose except my life, which isn't worth very much these days."

Layne rolled her eyes at Claire's melodramatic comment and playfully nudged her in Massie's direction.

Massie was standing by the bloody swimming pool, surrounded by a group of girls who were gushing over Bean's Dirty Devil costume. Four boys lingered on the outside of their tight circle, awkwardly punching each other.

Claire walked quickly at first but took smaller, slow steps once she entered Massie's force field.

"Hey there, co-host." Claire smiled as she nudged Massie's arm. She knew that was probably a bad idea as soon as she did it.

"S'cuse me," Massie said to her guests. She backed away from the circle and yanked Claire with her.

"What?" Massie barked when they were alone. The thick coating of black lipstick around Massie's mouth made her look so evil, Claire wondered if she was really in hell.

"Sorry to interrupt you, but I was wondering if—"

"Kuh-laire, do we look like a pair of boobs?"

"What?" Claire asked. "No."

"Then stop trying to hang beside me," Massie said.

"I was, uh, wondering if you could introduce us to a few

of the Briarwood boys?" Claire pointed to Layne, who was watching from the azaleas.

Massie straightened the horns on her head before she spoke. "Why don't you ask the couch poo? She knows the same people as me."

"She's shy," Claire said. "Besides, our moms were probably expecting you to help me out since they think we're such good friends and everything. Right? Isn't that what you told them when you asked if we could throw this party *together?*"

Claire prayed that her voice was trembling. "How upset do you think they'll be when they find out you've been telling everyone this is *your* party?"

"Why guess?" Massie asked. "Why not tell them right now?"

Claire's insides froze. That was not the answer she was hoping for.

"Fine, I will." Claire turned and headed down the path toward the main house. She looked down at her patent leather Mary Janes while she walked and prayed for a miracle. She had no idea what to do next, but she marched ahead like a girl with a serious plan.

"Okay, wait," Massie called after her.

Thank you, God!

"Meet me in the out-of-order bathroom in five minutes. I'll bring over two guys that I think will be perfect for you and Layne."

"No LBRs," Claire said. She knew she shouldn't abuse

her sudden power over Massie, but it was hard not to. "And no funny business or I'll talk."

"Done," Massie said.

As Claire walked back to Layne, she wondered if any boy was actually worth this kind of trouble.

When Hell Freezes Over Party

Out-of-Order Bathroom

8:22 PM

October 31st

The out-of-order bathroom was a tight squeeze for Layne and her oversized costume, so Claire was forced to sit on the toilet seat.

"I can't believe I let you talk me into this," Layne said.

"You promised." Claire finger-combed her blond hair and reapplied some clear gloss. "How many guys do you think will be into a girl they met on the toilet?" she asked Layne as she lowered herself onto the cold seat.

"We're being set up." Layne tried to keep the corners of her costume from scratching the plaid Ralph Lauren wallpaper. "Why would she have us wait in a *bathroom* if she wasn't planning something humiliating?"

"Trust me." Claire crossed her legs and bit into a Nerds Rope. "She just wanted us to meet her here so no one sees her talking to us in public."

"Oh, *that's* all." Layne shook her head. "Great, I feel sooo much better now."

She adjusted her pillows. "You know, meeting boys in bathrooms is something runaways do. I feel like we're being filmed for some sort of public service announcement."

They were interrupted by a light tapping on the bathroom door.

"Someone's in here," Claire shouted.

"No, it's *me,* Massie."

"Oh, come on in." Claire jumped to her feet. She was about to pinch her cheeks so she'd have a little color until she remembered her face was covered by a mask.

Massie tried to open the door and it jammed into Layne's costume.

"This is stupid," Layne snapped as she regained her balance. "I'm leaving."

She had managed to wiggle past Claire and get halfway out the door when she came face-to-face with two tall, gangly, dark-haired boys. One was surrounded by a chunk of gray foam and the other was in all black with dinner rolls pinned to his clothes.

"I'm Rock," said the chunk. "And he's Roll."

"Have a blast," Massie said. She turned and walked out of the cabana.

"Oh my God, that's hilarious," Layne said to the rock. She tried to slap her knee, but all she could do was lift her arm half an inch into the air and then lower it. "Can you guess what I am?"

"Of course," Rock said. "You're a couch potato. I've been watching you try to walk in that thing all night. You must be *fried.*"

Roll cracked up at his friend's potato joke and high-fived him.

"Oh my God, *fried,*" Layne said. "Claire, how funny is that?"

But Claire didn't think it was funny at all. She was more interested in why Massie assumed *she* would be into the garage band type. Layne might be "indie," but Claire was pure pop.

"I'm Eli," Rock said to Layne. "And this is Tristan."

"Hi," Claire and Layne said at the same time.

"Anyone wanna go for a skate?" Eli asked.

"Totally!" Layne said. "By the way, you rock."

"Could she be any BOULDER?" Claire said to Tristan, hoping her dorky pun would break the tension between them.

"Huh?" he said.

Claire didn't bother repeating herself. Instead she watched Layne and Eli take off toward the skating rink. She was embarrassed to have positioned herself as the "boy expert" when it took Layne less than ten minutes to meet her indie soul mate. Meanwhile, Claire would rather have been left with her own brother than Tristan.

"Wanna dance?" he asked.

"Uh, sure?" she said. But it came out sounding more like a question than an answer.

Tristan held his hand out to Claire. His nails shimmered with silver polish. They matched the silver sparkles in his blue eyeliner. Claire bent down and pretended to adjust the strap on her Mary Janes to avoid his gesture.

"Where do you get your makeup?" Claire asked once she straightened up.

"My older sister." Tristan looked proud. "I usually sneak into her room after she leaves for school."

"Usually?" Claire asked. "You mean it's not part of your costume?"

Tristan raised one eyebrow and cocked his head.

"When was the last time *you* saw a roll wearing eyeliner?"

Claire searched his face for signs that he might be joking, but he held her gaze.

The DJ put on Pink's "Get the Party Started" and Claire was grateful for the distraction.

"Oh, I love this song," she said. "Let's go."

Claire led the way, figuring a dance with Tristan was better than standing alone. But the second they got on the floor, Tristan started flailing around like a mental patient trying to shimmy his way out of a straitjacket. At first she tried to overlook his mania, but once the dinner rolls starting flying off his costume, she found him impossible to ignore.

"What are you doing?" Claire asked.

Claire's moves were more understated than usual. People were *already* staring, and she didn't want to attract any extra attention to herself. The only thing she was grateful for was that Massie wasn't around to witness this spectacle.

"Tristan, if you move any faster, you'll experience time travel," Claire said.

But he didn't hear her. He was too busy expressing himself. Claire decided no dance was worth this kind of embarrassment. So she backed away to the beat and made a run for the treats table.

WHEN HELL FREEZES OVER PARTY

PITS OF DESPAIR

8:40 PM

October 31st

"I am *dying* for marshmallows," Massie said to no one in particular. She lowered Bean onto the grass near the pit where Cam, Derrington, and Vader were hanging.

"Me too," Dylan said.

"Same," Alicia said.

"Sorry to crash, but this pit is theee best for roasting." Massie smiled at the boys. "I heard it has something to do with the wind."

"No problem," Vader said. He sat up straight and smoothed his gorilla fur.

Massie stuck three marshmallows on the prongs of her pitchfork and held them over the raging bonfire. She was standing between Alicia and Dylan, who were doing the same. They looked like three boys at a urinal.

Derrington, Cam, and their friend Vader sat on blankets below them. They were ripping handfuls of grass out of the ground and staring at the girls' Kiss It undies.

"I love watching a girl do a guy's work," Derrington said. He lay back and folded his hands behind his head.

His shaggy blond hair and brown eyes made Massie think of a yellow Lab.

"Well, that's what happens when there are no real guys around," Massie said.

The girls exchanged high fives.

"You're burnt, dude." Cam laughed. "She got you on that one." He rolled over, laughing.

Massie fought the smile that started to form on her face. She didn't want Cam to know his approval made her happy, even though it did.

"Shut up." Derrington pelted a marshmallow at Cam's cheek.

"Owww!" Cam shot one back.

Within seconds all six of them were engaged in a marshmallow war, which got particularly ugly when the girls started throwing the burning hot ones fresh off the fire.

"Ow, my neck," Cam screamed at Massie. He peeled a gooey marshmallow off his throat. He had to shake it three times before it finally flew off his fingers and landed on the grass.

"You're dead," he said.

Cam tore open a brand-new bag and launched a full-scale attack. He might be rail thin, but he was tall and strong and never missed his target.

The hailstorm of marshmallows was blinding, so Massie threw the rest of hers with her eyes closed. She never saw the waiter dressed as Satan's helper get hit on the cheek or the karate guy take one on the back. But she wouldn't have felt bad about it even if she had.

Massie heard her cell phone ringing.

"Time out," she said.

"Hullo?" She was out of breath. "It's Kristen," she mouthed to her friends.

"How's it going? We totally miss you, KRISTEN." Massie snuck a peek at Derrington to see if he perked up when he heard her name. She was dying to know which one of her friends he actually liked.

"Does anyone wanna say hi to KRISTEN?" Massie held out the phone in Derrington's general direction.

Vader made slurpy wet kissing sounds in Derrington's ear.

"Get away from me." Derrington squirmed and pushed Vader.

"Let *me* talk." Dylan grabbed the phone out of Massie's hand. "Hey, I heard you were bawling your eyes out earlier—are you okay?" She was speaking loud enough for the boys to hear. "Yeah, I can't believe you got GROUNDED. . . . I used to get GROUNDED a lot when I was a kid, but now that I'm *older,* I *never* get GROUNDED."

Alicia whipped a marshmallow at Dylan's head and the whole group cracked up.

"Derrick, stop it." Dylan laughed into the phone.

"It wasn't *me*—it was Alicia," Derrington said.

But it didn't matter. Dylan dropped the phone on the ground and opened fire on Derrington.

No one ever said goodbye to Kristen.

"This is boring," Alicia said suddenly. "Who wants to play spin the bottle?"

"I will," Vader answered quickly.

"By the way, why do they call you Vader?" Massie asked, trying to delay the kissing. She hated that Alicia was an expert on something she had never even tried. She didn't want to be called a prude at her own party.

"Have you ever heard him breathe?" Cam said.

Massie laughed harder than she needed to.

"Anyone else want to play?" Alicia asked. But no one answered. "Come on, you guys, it'll be fun."

"I'll play."

Everyone turned around to see where the mysterious voice came from.

A gorgeous girl stood alone by the pit. The dancing orange light from the fire lit her blue eyes beautifully. Her blond wavy hair touched the middle of her back. She looked like the kind of girl that belonged on a beach in California—the fact that she was dressed as a surfer girl (in a super-tight wet suit, of course) probably had something to do with that.

"Yeah, me too," Derrington said suddenly. "I'll play."

"Count me in," Cam added.

"Oh, *now* they want to play," Dylan said to Massie under her breath.

"Cool," the girl said, her eyes flickering in the flames. "It's great to see you guys, by the way."

"Yeah, great to see you too," Massie said. She turned to Dylan and shrugged. She had no idea who the stranger was.

"Ehmagod," Alicia said. "Olivia Ryan! I didn't recognize you. Where have you been all semester?"

"I was super sick," Olivia said. "But I'm much better now." It sounded like she was whispering, but she wasn't. Her voice had always been incredibly soft.

Dylan coughed, *"Nose job!"*

"Totally!" Massie coughed back.

"You look ah-mazing," Alicia said.

"Yeah, *different* somehow." Massie was trying to figure out who Olivia reminded her of.

Dylan gently elbowed Massie in the ribs and giggled. They looked at Alicia to see if she had noticed Olivia's surgically enhanced face, but if she did, she wasn't showing it.

"All right, who's ready to play?" Alicia asked the group. She seemed more into *having* fun with Olivia than *making* fun of her, which Massie found utterly puzzling.

"I am." Olivia raised her hand.

"I'm going to round up more people," Alicia said.

"Yay!" Olivia clapped. "I'll help."

The two girls linked arms and headed off toward the dance floor.

"Who does she remind me of?" Dylan asked Massie.

"No idea," she said. "I was wondering the same thing."

But Massie had bigger issues on her mind. If word got out that Olivia Ryan had more boy experience than Massie, she'd never live it down. She was minutes away from facing a swarm of lip-hungry seventh graders and a spinning bottle, and she was desperate to stop the game.

She pulled out her cell phone.

MASSIE: LKS LIKE DERRINGTON WANTZ 2 KISS OLIVIA.
DYLAN: ☹ HLP!
MASSIE: U GOT 2 STOP THE GAME.
DYLAN: ????
MASSIE: OLIVIA'S GERMS.☺
DYLAN: GOT IT. ☺

Dylan slipped her cell phone back in its Louis Vuitton case and then leaned in to Derrington and Cam and said, "I'm not so sure it's a good idea to play spin the bottle with someone who's been out for half a semester with a mysterious, face-altering sickness."

"Ehmagod," Massie said. "Ah-mazing point."

"Yeah, but her sickness made her look better than she did before," Vader said.

"For now," Massie said. "Who knows what kind of long-term effects this thing may have?" Massie watched Olivia swipe an empty Perrier bottle off the treats table and knew time was running out.

"I vote for health," Dylan said to Derrington. She lifted her palm in the air.

"Me too," Massie said. "I say we make a run for the out-of-order bathroom and hide there. It's way more private." She raised her eyebrows like a sexy seductress from the movies when she said "private." Massie had no idea how she'd keep kissing off the agenda, but she had another minute or so to figure it out.

"I'm game," Cam said with a devious smile. Massie could smell the grape Big League Chew he was chomping on and leaned in closer to get another whiff.

"What about you?" Dylan asked Derrington.

"Sure," he mumbled. "Let's go."

Derrington always mumbled, so it was hard for Massie to figure out if he was bored or excited. Either way, he went.

"Oh, so you're just going to leave me here to inhale Olivia's germs?" Vader shouted after them. "That's great. Thanks."

"Do you think Vader's really mad?" Dylan whispered to Derrington.

"Nah, he has Alicia and Olivia all to himself now," Derrington said. "He'll probably thank us."

Dylan, unhappy with Derrington's response, ate three Chunky chocolate squares on their short walk across the lawn. It was the first time Massie had seen her break her raw food diet all week.

"Where do you think *you're* going, gorgeous?"

Massie stopped walking and looked over her shoulder. Two boys in dresses were standing behind her. The one wearing the black wig was so tiny and frail he reminded Massie of the porcelain dolls she used to collect.

"We heard there was a spin-the-bottle game over at the pit," Todd said. "Care for an escort?" He offered Massie his elbow.

His tiny friend giggled. But it sounded more like a squeak.

"Shouldn't you nice ladies be looking for some *boys* to kiss?" Massie said.

Cam and Derrington cracked up.

"Excuse us, miss," Dylan said. She pulled Massie away and they made a run for the cabana.

They slipped into the bathroom and Cam shut the door behind them. His Drakkar Noir cologne hung in the air and Massie fought the urge to hug him. She casually waved her wrist around, hoping he'd find her Chanel No.19 just as enchanting.

"I wonder how dark it gets in here with the lights off?" Cam said. His soft, sweet voice made him sound curious instead of perverted.

He flicked the switch and the tiny bathroom turned pitch black. Massie could feel herself starting to panic. Her heart raced and her hands got clammy.

OMG! What if he makes a move?

"Check this out," Massie said. She turned a dial on the wall. A bulb in the ceiling lit up and the whole room glowed red. "Isn't that cool? It's a heat lamp. Now it really looks like hell in here."

There was a chorus of "ooh's" and "whoa's" followed by an awkward moment of silence. Dylan decided to make it worse.

"Is it true you have a crush on someone in our grade?" Dylan asked Derrington. She nervously turned the faucet on and off while she waited for his answer.

"What?"

"I heard you've had a crush on Kristen ever since the OCD benefit last month," she asked. "Is it true?"

Dylan's strategy was risqué. Massie was impressed.

"Well, I—," Derrington started to say. But he was interrupted.

"DIE, MORTALS! DIIIIIIIIEEEEE!" Alicia and Olivia burst through the bathroom door, making scary faces.

Dylan, Derrington, Massie, and Cam grabbed on to each other and screamed louder than any of them ever thought they could.

"Get 'em!" Cam shouted. He pushed his way past Massie and ran after Alicia and Olivia, who took off screaming and laughing. Derrington followed.

Dylan was speechless. She watched Olivia sprint across the lawn in her super-tight wet suit, turning heads with every stride she took.

"Well, *someone* likes getting chased by boys," Massie said to Dylan as they watched the sultry brunette and her new blond sidekick make off with their crushes.

"*Who* does she remind me of?" Dylan asked.

"I know," Massie said. "One of those Steve Madden models. You know, with the big heads and the skinny bodies."

"That's it!"

"Oh, and something else."

"What?"

"Dead meat."

When Hell Freezes Over Party

Treats Table

9:25 PM

October 31st

Claire stood at the edge of the ice rink, watching Layne skate and flirt with a guy dressed as a rock. She was so over standing on the sidelines, watching other people have fun.

It wasn't until Layne skated over a Reese's peanut butter cup and went flying through the air that Claire actually cracked a smile. She felt guilty right away for finding mild pleasure in her friend's accident, but she couldn't help it. Layne didn't even *want* to meet a boy, *she* did, and it wasn't fair! Somehow Layne's embarrassing wipeout made everything feel right again. Besides, the cushions around her neck broke the fall, so she wasn't hurt, just humiliated.

Eli tried helping Layne up. But their costumes kept colliding, so he couldn't get a strong grip on her arm. After several failed attempts Layne crawled toward land.

"Hey there, Blossom."

Claire heard the tiny voice and turned to find Nathan looking up at her, his green dress covered in chocolate stains.

"Hi, Buttercup," she said softly. There was something about being around such a petite guy that made everyone use their small voice when they spoke to him. "Where's Bubbles?"

"He's hiding in the bushes, throwing Smarties at Massie."

Claire slowly shook her head.

"Wanna go get drawn by the caricature guy?" Nathan asked.

"Sure. Why not?"

Claire knew her social life had reached an all-time low as she strolled across the lawn with her brother's midgety friend.

They found the artist on the stone porch beside the side entrance of the house.

When he saw Blossom and Buttercup approach, he slapped his hand against his heart and smiled.

"Now, aren't you two precious," he said. "Come. Sit, sit, sit."

"Are you sure you want to do this?" she mumbled to Nathan.

"Yes," he squeaked.

"Howdy," the artist said. "I'm Jules Denver."

Claire noticed his dry, chalky hands as he extended his arm to greet her. She shook it politely, then wiped her palm on the side of her dress when he wasn't looking.

Jules had gray feathered hair that Claire assumed had been blown dry by a professional. His nose was big and bulbous and his deep set eyes were tiny slits. Claire thought Jules's extreme features looked like one of the sample caricatures wrapped in plastic, tacked to the side of his easel.

"I think it would be darling if your little friend sat on your lap for the portrait," he said to Claire.

"Do you think that will make me look like a ventriloquist?" Claire asked in her kindest voice. "Maybe I should just stand behind him."

"What-*ever.*" Jules's smile faded. "Please look over there." He pointed his red Magic Marker at the big oak tree with the dangling mannequin. "And don't move."

Five girls dressed as mice stood under the tree in a tight cluster, talking to each other with their hands over their mouths. Claire was trying to read their lips when she saw a cute guy with messy black hair, dressed as a soccer goalie, run past them. He was looking over his shoulder as if he was being chased. But no one was behind him.

"Maybe he's had too much sugar," Claire said to Nathan. But Nathan didn't respond.

"No talking," Jules snapped.

Claire wished Layne was around because she would have found that funny.

"Look straight at the tree, dear," Jules said.

Every time Jules looked down at his paper, Claire tried to spot Cute Running Guy without moving her face. Finally she found him. He was heading her way.

"Look out," Claire said to Jules.

But it was too late. Cute Running Guy slammed straight into Jules, sending him face-first onto his easel.

"Medic," Jules said. He lay flat on the ground, surrounded by Magic Markers.

"Sorry, man," Cute Running Guy said as he lifted himself off Jules. "I didn't see you there."

Claire and Nathan fought the urge to laugh for as long as they possibly could.

"Very funny," Jules said to Claire with a snarl. "I think I broke my hip."

"We should probably go," Claire said as she backed away. "Feel better."

Blossom, Buttercup, and the soccer player broke into a fit of hysteria as soon as Jules was out of earshot.

"Sorry I ruined your picture," the soccer player said.

"Are you kidding?" Claire said. "You saved my life."

"Good." He smiled. Claire liked his soft voice and had the sudden urge to hear him say her name the same way he just said "good."

"I'm Claire," she said. "And this is my brother's friend Nathan." She pointed to the ground, but no one was there. "Oh, well, that *was* Nathan. Funny, I didn't see him leave."

"I'm Cam," he said. His black hair and red lips made Claire think of Snow White but in a total guy way.

"Who were you running from?" Claire asked.

"These two girls, Alicia and Olivia. But I think I lost them."

"Is that a good thing?" Claire asked.

Please say yes please say yes.

"Yes." He sighed. "I mean, they're cool and everything, but they're a little hyper for me, you know?"

"They are a lot of things. All of which are worth running from."

Cam chuckled. His eyes laughed.

"Are you having fun at my party?" Claire asked.

"This is *your* party? I thought it was Massie's."

Claire fought the urge to sound bitter. "We threw it together," she said. "I live right over there." She pointed to the small stone house with the cutout cardboard ghosts taped to the door.

"Oh, no way." He sounded surprised. "So *you're* the new girl."

"Yyyy-eah." She couldn't tell what he was going to do next.

But he didn't do anything except stare at her with his different color eyes.

"What?" Claire tugged at the hair elastic around her wrist until it pinched her skin.

"I heard about you, that's all," he said. "Don't worry, it was all good."

Claire was dying to ask him *what* he had heard, *who* he'd heard it from, and *when* he'd heard it. But she didn't want to seem desperate.

"Nice," was all she said.

After an awkward silence Cam spoke.

"Massie seems fun. I hung out with her at the benefit and I thought she was pretty cool—you know, for an OCD girl." He gently punched her arm.

Claire giggled.

"I was at that party," she said. "But you must have been too busy flirting with Massie to notice."

Cam stuffed his hands in the pockets of his shorts and smiled shyly.

"Looks like someone has a bit of a crush on Massie Block."

Claire hoped he wouldn't pick up on her disappointment.

But she'd never know because he wiped a wavy mass of hair out of his eyes and changed the subject immediately. He looked toward the dance floor, where everyone was clapping and cheering for a half-naked chubby guy who was twirling his shirt above his head to the beat of the music.

"Wanna see what's going on over there?"

"Sure," Claire said. "But I can't promise I'll like it."

Cam laughed and Claire smiled. She was glad he shared her sense of humor and she wanted him to know it. In fact, she wanted him to know a lot of things about her, but if he liked Massie, he probably liked girls who played hard to get. Claire decided to act slightly bored while they danced.

"Happy Halloween, everyone!" the DJ shouted. "Are you having fun tonight?" The crowd "woo-ed" and clapped. "I have one song left and I wanna make it count. Can you handle it?"

Fists shot into the air and everyone was throwing handfuls of candy around.

"I thought so." He flashed his cheesy DJ smile. "I've got two gift certificates to iTunes right here for the couple with the best moves." He held two white envelopes above his head.

"Those are ours," Cam said to Claire. He wiped his palms on his soccer shorts.

After the first beat of Nelly's "Hot in Herre" the crowd exploded. Their cumbersome masks, tails, hats, capes, and shoes were tossed to the side of the dance floor.

Tired parents, stuck with the late night carpool shift,

started to trickle in. They didn't dare drag their kids out before the final song had ended so they talked among themselves with their arms folded and their car keys in hand.

Claire, desperate to impress, threw in a few leaps from gymnastics and some butt-shaking dance moves she copied from music videos. She was so focused she had to remind herself to look up and see what Cam was doing. When he wasn't looking, she wiped the sweat from her forehead and checked him out.

He looked like an outlaw from the old Western movies her father and Todd liked to watch. His hands were out in front of him and his fingers were pointing straight ahead like guns. Each time the music pulsed, Cam would "fire" the guns with his thumbs. He moved to the beat without ever lifting his feet off the ground.

Todd and Nathan were running around, pushing each other into pretty girls. As soon as one of them slammed into someone, they'd take off before the girl or the guy she was dancing with could spot them.

Dylan, Alicia, and some blond girl Claire had never seen before were on the opposite end of the dance floor surrounded by a group of gyrating boys. Claire saw them glance at her a few times and point to Cam. She could tell they were impressed by her partner, which inspired her to dance even better. If only Massie had been around to see her. But she was nowhere in sight. Hopefully Dylan and Alicia would spread the word.

The music stopped and the parents looked relieved.

"And the winner of tonight's When Hell Freezes Over dance contest is—" The DJ played a drumroll sound effect. "The soccer player and the Powerpuff Girl."

The disappointed crowd applauded politely.

Todd and Nathan looked surprised but flattered as they made their way toward the DJ booth to collect their prize.

"What are *you* doing here?" Claire asked her brother.

"I've come for what's rightfully mine," he said. Nathan reached his tiny hand across Cam and grabbed at the white envelopes the DJ was holding.

"Get away from me, you little rodent," the DJ said. He held the gift certificates above his head and out of Nathan's reach.

"Leave or I'm not doing your math homework," Claire whispered to Todd.

"Hey, Nathan, look! There's candy all over the ground," Todd said.

And off they went.

Cam was so happy he hugged Claire in front of everyone. He was even more grateful when she gave him her gift certificate.

"Are you sure?" Cam asked as he took the piece of paper from Claire's clammy hand.

"Positive. I don't have an iPod." But Claire knew she would have given it to him even if she did. She would have done anything to make him smile at her that way.

"Well, I'll make you a killer mix of all the songs I download." Cam stuffed the envelopes deep in his pocket.

"I should go," he said. "Thanks for the party. It was fun."

"Cool," was the only thing Claire could think of to say. She reached into the side of her kneesock and pulled out her digital camera. Cam was already a few feet away, and his back was to her, but she quickly snapped his picture anyway.

Friends hugged each other goodbye while their parents roamed the yard, picking up familiar costume parts.

Massie was at the gate saying "good night" and "you're welcome" to her guests, who all praised her for hosting such an incredible party. No one stopped to thank Claire. But she didn't let that put a damper on her night, which had ended up perfect thanks to Cam. She couldn't wait to tell Layne she was no longer a "Mopey Dick."

When everyone was finally gone, Claire took off her red wig and started heading toward the guesthouse. She couldn't wait to take a shower and crawl into bed.

"Where do you think *you're* going?" Massie called after her. She was putting on a pair of yellow rubber gloves and holding a big green garbage bag. "My mom said we have to throw out the food so the raccoons don't invade."

"*Now* I'm a co-host?" Claire said. The crisp wind dried the sweat on her body and she felt cold for the first time all night.

"Landon was supposed to take care of this, but she's gone," Massie said. "We must have run out of coffee or something."

Claire sighed. She slid the elastic off her wrist and put her hair in a high ponytail.

They walked across the lawn side by side, picking up smushed chocolate, crushed cups, and costume scraps.

When Massie bent down to pick up a rubber nose, Claire stole a quick glance at the picture she took of Cam. She didn't get a shot of his face, but his calf muscles looked cute. She couldn't wait to e-mail the picture to her friends back in Florida.

"So what'd you think of that guy?" Massie asked Claire.

"I really like him," Claire said. She could feel herself turning red.

"I'm not surprised," Massie said. "You guys have the same taste in makeup."

"Huh?"

"And it looked like Layne and Eli totally hit it off too," Massie continued. "I saw them trying to kiss each other good night, but their costumes kept bumping, so they never made contact."

Claire realized Massie was talking about Tristan, not Cam. She decided not to correct her. The less Massie knew, the safer Claire would be.

"What about you?" Claire asked. "Any crushes tonight?"

"Nah." Massie shook her head vigorously. "I was busy making sure my friends didn't kill each other. I spent half the night on the phone listening to Kristen cry over some doof who wears shorts in the winter. I even missed the dance contest."

Claire was about to blurt that she'd won but stopped herself at the last minute.

"You're so lucky you don't have friends," Massie said. "Sometimes they can be so depressing."

"I have tons of friends in Florida, you know," Claire said.

But Massie didn't respond. She was too busy peeling a smushed marshmallow off the treats table.

"I can't believe Alicia and Olivia left without saying goodbye to me," Massie said as she tossed an empty bottle of Pellegrino into her garbage bag.

"Who's Olivia?"

Massie seemed too wrapped up in her own thoughts to explain.

"Oh, well." She sighed. "You know, friends are like clothes—they can't be *in* forever."

"That's the saddest thing I've ever heard," Claire mumbled to herself.

"What?"

"Nothing, I was singing."

Claire wanted to ask Massie if she really meant that but didn't bother. She already knew the answer.

OCTAVIAN COUNTRY DAY SCHOOL
SAGAMORE HALL
9:00 AM
November 3rd

"What can this emergency assembly *possibly* be about?" Massie whispered to Kristen.

It had been an amazing weekend, filled with leftover Halloween candy and postparty gossip. And no one was in the mood for a Monday morning lecture. The seventh graders were making their way down the carpeted aisle of the school auditorium. Massie and her friends were at the very back of the line.

"I heard it has to do with Dori's petition," Kristen said. "Supposedly it upset the cafeteria ladies 'cause it said they should get manicures before serving food to minors. And everyone signed."

"*Someone* had to tell them." Massie pulled the bottom of her hair toward her nose so she could get a whiff of her Aveda shampoo. It had been a while since the doors to Sagamore Assembly Hall had been cracked, and the smell of stale carpet hung in the air.

Principal Burns stood by the stage and held open the infamous velvet satchel. One by one, the girls gently placed their phones inside before taking their seats. The "cell block" was the principal's most recent effort to silence the symphony of ringing phones that interrupted every assembly. It also meant everyone had to suffer through her boring speeches without the distraction of text messages. Massie always made sure hers was the very last one in the bag so it wouldn't get scuffed.

On the way to her seat, Massie loosened the pink, gray, and purple cashmere scarves around her neck and wondered if Claire had as much trouble with the bet that morning as she had. She scanned the room and half smiled to herself when she saw two wanna-bes in the hideous red-and-mustard-yellow combo she was forced to wear during her walk of shame on Friday. It seemed like everyone was searching for fashion inspiration. Massie had a feeling Claire found hers in Layne's attic. The patch suede seventies skirt and the yellow Feelin' Groovy T-shirt she wore were dead giveaways.

Massie pulled down a cushioned theater seat and sat between Kristen and Dylan. They had purposely left a space between them so they wouldn't have to sit together.

Alicia arrived but barely uttered a word to any of them. She was too busy snickering with her new BFF Olivia about all the e-mails they got from Derrington that weekend.

"And how about that thing he does with all his D's?" Alicia said.

"You mean how they're all in red?" Olivia asked. "Yeah, what's up with that? Do you think there's something wrong with his computer?"

"No. It's 'cause his name starts with D and he's trying to be cute." Alicia sounded confused, like she couldn't tell if Olivia was serious or not.

Massie rolled her eyes. She couldn't believe Olivia was such a ditz and wondered why Alicia didn't make fun of her. Normally Massie would have asked, but she was giving Alicia the silent treatment for not saying goodbye after the party.

Everyone was fighting.

Kristen was giving Dylan the stink eye for flirting with Derrington when she called during the Halloween party. Dylan was mad at Kristen for liking Derrington even though they barely knew each other. And they were both mad at Alicia for e-mailing Derrington even though Alicia claimed *he* started it. Everyone could have been mad at Olivia too, but no one liked her enough to bother.

"Ladies, it's time to simmer," Principal Burns announced as she adjusted the microphone on the wooden podium at the front of the room. She scanned the room, using only her beady eyes while keeping the rest of her body completely motionless. Everyone thought she looked like a buzzard.

"I'll get right to the point," Principal Burns said. "Last week some serious violations were brought to my attention."

Massie craned her neck to see Dori's reaction. Just as Massie suspected, the girl was smiling proudly, like she just won on *American Idol.*

Why didn't I think of doing a petition?

"What started out as a few attention-starved girls prancing around in tasteless outfits spread through the halls of our school like a virus," Principal Burns declared. "And by lunchtime the entire grade was rated R for full frontal nudity."

Dori's smile faded. Massie's lit up.

Massie reached for her cell phone so she could fire off an "OMG!" to Kristen and Dylan, but it was in the velvet basket.

Ugh!

Forced to communicate the old-fashioned way, Massie dug her nails into Kristen's thigh. Kristen responded by pinching Massie's arm.

"Soon thereafter, a pack of angry parents called an emergency board meeting, which lasted for five hours and kept me from seeing my only son in his VERY FIRST HALLOWEEN COSTUME—he was a little baby bird."

Massie, Kristen, Alicia, and Dylan quickly covered their mouths to conceal their laughter. A few other girls snickered but stopped as soon as Principal Burns seared them with her tiny black eyes.

After a dramatic pause and a deep inhalation she continued. "Eventually we came to a decision."

Dylan reached her arm across the back of her seat and gently grabbed a chunk of Massie's hair. Massie clutched the back of Dylan's crisp white collar. They couldn't imagine what was going to come out of Principal Burns's mouth, but they had a feeling it wasn't going to be good.

"It gives me great pain to announce—" She paused.

Murmurs and whispers grew out of every corner of the room. She cleared her throat and continued.

"OCD is going UNIFORM. The head of our fashion department, Pia Vogel, will fill you in on the details because frankly, I'm too upset to speak."

The assembly hall erupted into a chorus of "no way's!" and "not fair's," but Principal Burns cleared her throat in the microphone and the room was hers once again.

"I don't know who I'm more disappointed with, the girls who started this or the ones who followed them," she said as she backed away from the podium.

The sound of bodies shifting in their seats filled the room as the entire grade turned to find Massie. She felt a wave of prickly heat creep up her entire body. For the first time in her life she didn't want to be the girl everyone in the room was staring at. But unfortunately, she was.

OCTAVIAN COUNTRY DAY SCHOOL
TEACHERS' BATHROOM
10:01 AM
November 3rd

For the moment Massie was safe. The last stall in the teachers' private bathroom was the only thing that stood between her and a furious mob of seventh graders. She wasn't completely sure how much blame her classmates were going to place on her. She wasn't stupid enough to linger after the assembly to find out. As soon as Principal Burns clapped and dismissed everyone, Massie squeezed her way through the crowd and ducked out of the emergency exit undetected. She was so desperate to escape she left her cell in the basket, figuring she'd buy a new one after school. At least she had her PalmPilot. There was a lot that needed to be said.

CURRENT STATE OF THE UNION

IN	OUT
Alicia and Olivia	Massie, Kristen, Alicia, and Dylan
Uniforms	Freedom, self-expression, personal style
Massie, Wanted Dead or Alive	Me

Massie imagined being forced out of her table in the Café by a bunch of angry girls in uniforms and having to eat with the teachers for protection. She was fighting back the tears when the bathroom door opened and someone walked in. She stepped up on the toilet seat while gripping her bracelet so the charms wouldn't clang together and give her away.

She did her best to stay quiet and managed to avoid breathing for twenty-two seconds straight. The intruder wasn't using the toilet or the sink. She seemed to be hovering for no apparent reason.

Leave, she thought. *LEAVE!*

The standoff made Massie anxious. She hated being stalked and would have preferred getting caught to this nerve-racking, not to mention *bo-rrring,* exercise in endurance. She lowered herself off the toilet as slowly and silently as she could. Once both feet were on the ground, she held her hair back and bent down so she could take a peek under the stall.

She could feel the blood rush to her head as she hung her face upside down, but discomfort was the furthest thing from her mind. Especially once she saw what was on the other side.

"Ahhh!" Massie screamed when she saw the huge blue eye looking back at her.

"Ahhh!" the eye screamed back.

It didn't look like teacher eye because it didn't have any black mascara boogers floating in the corners.

"Open the door," the eye said.

Massie recognized that chipmunky voice. It was Claire.

"Is it safe?" Massie asked.

"Yes," Claire whispered. "All the teachers are outside, trying to break up the protest."

"Protest?"

"Yeah, Layne is leading a March for Uniform Reform. Come look. You can see it from the window."

Massie opened the door. She didn't bother looking outside.

"Does everyone want to kill me?" Massie asked.

"Gabby and Bella said something about finding you and hanging you from the flagpole by your three scarves, but I think you can take them. Kristen and Dylan are worried—"

"What about Alicia?" Massie asked. "Is she looking for me?" She immediately regretted the question.

"No," Claire said. "She's with Olivia at the Starbucks kiosk. I passed them on my way over here. By the way, I have your phone."

Claire carefully passed her the Motorola. Massie thought that was the most thoughtful thing anyone had ever done for her, but she said nothing.

"I came alone. You have nothing to worry about." Claire spoke as if she had just read Massie's mind. "I saw you sneak out of the emergency exit." Her smile was big and genuine. "Isn't it funny that you and I will be dressed the exact same every single day?"

Massie had to fight the urge to hurl her phone at Claire's head. If she hadn't spent three hours over the weekend gluing purple rhinestones to the front of it, she would have.

"I would rather keep our bet going for another year than wear the same stiff white shirt and itchy kilt as everyone else." Massie scratched her leg at the thought.

"You should design the uniforms," Claire said. "You have the best style in the school and you get straight A's in fashion class."

Massie could feel the blood rush back to her face. *What a perfect idea,* she thought. *Then everyone in the grade will be wearing something* I *created. I'll be a legend.*

Massie wondered what kind of logo she'd put on her label. Would it be a crown or a photo of Bean? Would her line be exclusive to OCD students or would she offer her creations to the masses? Would Cam be impressed?

"I'll talk to Pia about it," she said, trying to downplay her excitement. "I bet she'll let me. My parents donate so much money to OCD as it is. And if they want more, I can just ask my dad to build a design studio or something. By the way, why did you follow me here?" Massie asked.

"I dunno," Claire said. "I thought you could use a friend."

"*Puh-lease,* what's in it for you?"

"A friend."

Claire's answer was so pure and simple it caught Massie off guard. She folded her arms and squinted, searching for signs of insincerity on Claire's face. She couldn't find any.

"If you want, you can come over after school and help me think of some ideas." Massie was surprised to hear those words come out of her own mouth.

Claire looked as shocked. They both stood perfectly still, each wondering if she had imagined what Massie had said.

"You know, for our mothers, of course," Massie said. She

swung her Prada messenger bag over her shoulder. "Maybe you'll finally get a cell phone out of it."

"It's worth another try," Claire said.

Massie led the way out of the bathroom and onto the battlefield to fight for something she believed in very deeply: her personal style.

The Café
Starbucks Kiosk
2:04 PM
November 3rd

Massie waited for Alicia, Kristen, and Dylan to add the necessary amounts of Equal and cinnamon to their lattes before giving them the update.

"Requesting permission for twenty gossip points," she said, then casually blew on her chai tea.

"*Twenty* points?" Alicia screeched. "That means you either have a copy of our science test or Britney's getting married again and you scored us an invite."

"Britney Foster's getting *married?*" Olivia asked. "She's a grade below *us.*"

"NO, Britney Sp—"

"Isn't she sooo hilarious," Alicia jumped in. But no one was laughing.

"My news will be released to the public in an assembly tomorrow morning, but if you want to hear it now, it will cost you twenty," Massie said

"Done," Dylan said.

"Done," Kristen said.

"Done," Alicia said.

"Done," Olivia said.

"Is there an echo in here? I thought I heard an extra 'done.'" Massie looked around the Café. If she had been speaking to Alicia, she would have asked her why Olivia was there. "Anyway, after the assembly, while everyone was protesting—"

"Yeah, where *were* you? We were looking everywhere," Dylan said.

"I ran straight to Pia Vogel's office to have a *word* with her about the whole uniform thing." Massie decided to leave out the part about hiding in the bathroom.

"I hope your word was 'totally unfair,'" Olivia said.

"That's *two* words." Kristen rolled her eyes.

"Oh."

Massie didn't tell them she talked to Pia about designing the uniforms herself. Because Pia's answer was no. Massie only told them how the conversation ended.

"So after a lot of back and forth, Pia finally agreed to hold an OCD uniform design contest. She even said she'd call the editors at *Teen People* and ask them to do a story on the winner. There will be a fashion show on Saturday. That's when the voting will take place."

"How awesome!" Olivia clapped and bounced up and down. She stopped when she noticed no one else seemed excited.

"This week? That's totally unrealistic." Kristen rubbed her eyes. "How are we supposed to design something that quickly?"

"I know, it sucks, but they want to start the uniform thing ASAP," Massie explained. "I tried to fight it, but Pia wouldn't budge."

"This whole thing sucks," Kristen said. "The last thing I need is more homework this week."

"Yeah." Dylan frowned. "I have over thirty hours of unwatched shows piling up on my TiVo. Now I have to learn how to sew?"

Massie was determined to sell them on the idea since she was responsible for the entire mess.

She laughed out loud.

"What's so funny?" Alicia asked. "They're right—this whole thing blows."

"You guys crack me up," Massie said. "I love when you do that thing where you pretend to miss the point. I fall for it every time."

Olivia looked relieved.

"I mean, Kristen, you of all people must be psyched about this. You'll never have to switch outfits in the car on the way to school ever again. If you design the winning outfit and it becomes the school uniform, your mother will *have* to let you wear it," Massie said. Kristen's navy blue eyes sparkled at the very idea.

"And Dylan, Philippe, your mom's wardrobe guy, can help you. You won't even have to touch a piece of fabric."

Massie could tell her friends were warming up to the idea.

"Alicia, the other day you said you wished more people dressed like you. If you win this contest, everyone *will.*"

That was the first time Massie spoke directly to Alicia all morning.

"When I left Pia, she was ordering T-shirts that said

OCD Puts the U in Uniform," Massie said. "She wants to give them out on the night of the show."

"It kind of sounds like fun," Dylan said.

"You deserve more than twenty points for this, Mass," Kristen said. "You saved us."

"It also means we only have a couple of weeks left to wear our new fall clothes." Alicia smiled.

"Speaking of which, I need to recall anything I've lent you in the last six months." Massie tightened her three scarves. "I'm desperate for something new to wear."

The girls nodded. Now if only Massie could get rid of Olivia and keep Derrington from coming between her friends. Just then, as if on cue, Alicia's cell phone vibrated.

"Look, it's from Derrington." Alicia tilted the tiny screen toward Olivia. "He wants to know what's up."

"How cute of him." Olivia gathered her long blond hair and tossed it behind her head.

Kristen and Dylan instinctively turned to each other to roll their eyes but looked away once they remembered they weren't speaking to each other.

"Massie, he's asking if you're around," Olivia said, looking at the screen.

Why couldn't it be Cam?

"Massie, he wants me to thank you for the party," Alicia relayed. "He had a blast."

"He already thanked me, so how 'bout I just credit that one to your account?" But Massie's clever comeback was lost on Alicia. She was busy typing and giggling with Olivia.

"He's sweet." Alicia snapped her phone shut. "I'm sure he'll make *one* of you very happy."

"Whatever, I don't want your sloppy seconds," Kristen said. "I'm going to get started on my design."

"Same," Dylan said. "I'm thinking of doing something reversible so it will be like having two uniforms instead of one."

"That's what I was going to do," Kristen said. "You heard me talking about that after the assembly, didn't you?"

"NO!" Dylan shouted. "I haven't listened to anything you've said all day."

Massie rolled her eyes as she gathered up her books. At least no one was mad at *her.* She knew she'd find a way to fix things and bring them all together again. She just needed a little time.

The bell rang and the girls tossed their cups in a nearby trash can.

"What are you going to design?" Dylan asked Massie.

"I'll figure it out in American history," she said. "I do some of my best scheming in that class."

It seemed like everyone had fallen for Derrington's unkempt good looks except Massie. How could anyone like a boy who *always* wore shorts, even in the winter? His kneecaps were constantly purple from the cold and for Massie, love could never be *that* blind. Cam, on the other hand, made his fashion statement with a beat-up motorcycle jacket. It was one of the many things he had inherited from his older brother, Harris, who was a senior at Briarwood. Cam's love of The Strokes, the Godfather movies, and soccer were also Harris hand-me-downs. But the jacket was his favorite. The worked-in brown leather was filled with cracks and oil stains, but Massie saw beyond the filth because the vintage piece was the perfect mix of rugged and soft. Just like Cam.

Bean was the only living creature that knew about Massie's crush. And she hated how pathetic Kristen and Dylan looked, fighting over a guy who didn't necessarily like either one of them. For the time being she would have to come up with an excuse to contact Cam all by herself.

After school, she found his e-mail address in her deleted messages folder and was glad she hadn't erased his RSVP from her files.

After twenty minutes of writing and erasing her message, she settled on:

HEY, CAM,

JUST WONDERING IF YOU LEFT A PAIR OF SHIN GUARDS HERE AFTER THE HALLOWEEN PARTY. RENNY WHITE WAS THE ONLY OTHER GUY DRESSED AS A SOCCER PLAYER AND I REALLY DON'T WANT TO CALL HIM 'CAUSE HIS VOICE SOUNDS LIKE SNUFFLEUPAGUS AND I LAUGH EVERY TIME I TALK TO HIM. ☺

—MB

Massie read the e-mail three times before sending it. She prayed Cam hadn't actually lost his shin guards because she didn't have any to give him.

Her e-mail dinged immediately and Massie's heart leapt. Cam had replied. Massie put on a thick coat of lip gloss and fluffed up her hair before opening it.

MB—

I HAVE MY SHIN GUARDS. THNX. I LOL'ED WHEN I READ ABOUT RENNY. I ALWAYS THOUGHT THAT TOO. HEY, THERE'S A RUMOR GOING AROUND THAT OCD IS GOING UNIFORM. TRUE? ALSO HEARD IT'S YOUR FAULT. IF IT IS, THAT'S PRETTY COOL.

I LIKE TROUBLEMAKERS. ☺

—C

"Oh my God, Bean," Massie gulped as she lifted her dog onto her lap. "He practically admitted he likes me! Now what?"

Massie hopped up from her chair and paced around her room, Bean still in her arms.

"It can't end like this. It may be weeks before I talk to him again. What if he forgets he likes me?"

The sound of Bean's panting kept Massie from feeling alone.

"I wish you could talk. But I guess if you could, I wouldn't tell you anything, so maybe it's better that you don't."

Massie sat back down in front of her computer and went for it.

IT'S A GREAT STORY. CALL ME IF YOU WANT TO HEAR IT. IF NOT, I'LL SEE YOU SOON.

—MB ☺

Massie was proud of her last response. It was an invitation for him to call her, but at the same time she made it seem like it didn't matter if he took her up on it.

Her phone rang seconds later. She answered.

"Hi, Massie?"

It was Cam.

"Are you eating?" Massie asked. "I can hear you chomping on something."

"It's Big League Chew."

"Grape?"

"Yeah," Cam said. "How did you know?"

"It's what you always chew."

Massie was so charged with energy she wanted to scream. She stopped pacing long enough to sit down at her computer and do a quick search on *The Godfather* just in case it came up (*a 1972 film directed by Francis Ford Coppola . . . zzz . . . zzz . . . zzz . . .*). Luckily it never did.

They talked about their classes, their families, and their favorite Web sites. He even asked what it was like having "the new girl" around all the time and said he "totally felt her pain" when she explained what a drag it was. There were only two awkward silences in the entire thirty-seven-minute conversation and he promised to make her a CD mix of his favorite Strokes songs. If his mother hadn't called him to dinner, they would have talked all night.

When Massie hung up the phone, she was ready to burst. Even though they made no solid plans to see each other (ugh!), Cam promised he would call her again and Massie believed him.

"Bean!" Massie hugged her dog. "I wish I could be friends with myself so I'd have someone to jump up and down with right now."

Massie closed her blinds to make sure Claire couldn't see into her bedroom and then hopped up on her bed. She jumped twice and let out a big "whoo-hoo," but that was the extent of her victory dance. She felt stupid celebrating alone.

The Block Estate
Living Room
6:36 PM
November 3rd

"If you want to work in the same room as me, you're going to have to set up behind there." Massie was pointing to the brown suede couch on the far side of the living room. "And I'll work behind this one."

Claire wasn't going to argue. She walked over to her couch and emptied her plastic bag of material on the cream-colored carpet. This was Claire's big chance to spend alone time with Massie and maybe, if things went well, she'd be *in* by the end of the night.

"So what's your uniform idea?" Claire felt weird talking to Massie with a piece of furniture between them.

"Do you seriously think I'm going to tell you?" Massie snapped. She didn't say it in a mean way, like, "Do you seriously think I'm going to tell *you?*" She sounded like she just wasn't going to tell *anyone.*

Ever since Pia announced the contest that morning, the entire grade became secretive and paranoid. Bathroom stalls were used as phone booths by girls who wanted privacy while talking to their "outside contacts." The Café was practically silent during lunch. It was like someone had accidentally hit mute on the otherwise bustling scene.

Claire thought about her old school in Orlando and felt a pang of sadness. There, a design contest would have had everyone running around sharing ideas and teaming up with partners. But at OCD, where the students were the kids of CEOs, politicians, and celebrities, no one cared about creativity or teamwork. They cared about winning.

Pia invited designers and dressmakers to teach sewing clinics and pattern-making workshops after school. And Claire signed up for them all. The extra studying would be worth it if she won the design contest and could hear herself being referred to as something other than "the new girl with Keds."

After the first workshop, called "Sew What?" Claire decided on a uniform that was all about comfort and simplicity, something she thought the overdressed OCD girls should finally consider. She wanted to make a velour skirt that would fasten with a pull string instead of a zipper. A hoodie, with the OCD Phoenix on the right side of the chest, would replace the blazer. T-shirts and sneakers would also be part of the comfy overall image. And of course everything would be in the school colors, navy blue and maroon. Claire was confident that once the seventh graders got a taste of casual dressing, they would thank her until the end of time.

For the next half hour the girls worked without talking, the only sound in the room the squeak of scissors cutting through fabric. After a while Claire peeked out over her couch. Massie was measuring her mannequin. She wore a pair of red Juicy Couture sweats and her hair was piled on top of her head. Even though she seemed ready for bed, Claire thought Massie looked pretty.

"I see you watching me," Massie said without even turning her head.

"Uh, I was just—"

"Claire, do you work at a grocery store?" Massie asked as she was wrapping her tape measure around her mannequin's waist.

"Huh? No," Claire said.

"Then why are you checking me out?"

Claire flopped back on the carpeted floor behind her designated couch and tried to make sense of the patterns that stared back at her. She wished Layne could help, but she had already joined forces with Eli.

Layne had invited Claire to team up with them, but Claire had politely declined the offer when she heard their plan. Layne wanted Eli to be her model.

"Are you serious?" Claire asked them. They were in an art supply store after school, waiting for Eli to decide on a sketch pad.

"Claire, uniforms strip away our freedom of expression by forcing everyone to look identical," Eli explained. He flipped opened an Utrecht notebook and rubbed a sheet of thick paper between his thumb and index finger.

Claire was trying really hard to pay attention, but all

she could focus on was Eli's chipped navy blue nail polish.

"So we're taking that idea one step further by saying why not make *all* of us look the same, boys included," Eli said. He looked at the price sticker on the inside of the notebook and put it back on the shelf.

"Isn't that genius?" Layne looked really proud.

The only words Claire could think of at that moment were dripping with sarcasm, so she stuffed her mouth with the last of her gummy supply to keep herself quiet.

"Did you hear that Eli is going to be Layne's model?" Claire asked from behind her couch.

"No way!" Massie shouted back from her side of the room. "Is she really?"

"You mean *he?*"

"No, I meant *she.*" Massie giggled.

Claire laughed too.

By the time they had finished listening to John Mayer, Beyoncé, and No Doubt, Claire had managed to make sense of her pattern instructions. Her first incision was a success, and as time passed, she started to relax and enjoy herself. Hours flew by while the girls worked.

Claire was admiring her finished skirt when Massie's phone rang.

"Hey, Alicia," Massie said.

Claire thought Massie sounded cold toward her friend and wondered if she was still mad about the whole Alicia-leaving-the-party-without-saying-goodbye thing.

"What's up?" Massie asked as she turned down the volume on the stereo. "Yeah, I think Derrington's cool, I guess. . . . Why? . . . Did you find out if he likes Dylan yet? . . . What about Kristen? . . . Is he *ever* going to tell you? . . . Well, what about Cam? . . . Does he like anyone?"

Claire stopped sewing. She leaned against the back of the couch and listened.

"No, I don't like *Cam.*" Massie started pacing around the living room. "I was just asking 'cause I thought maybe Olivia did. . . . Well, she was chasing him around at the party a lot. . . . Cam *likes* someone?"

"Who?" Claire mouthed to herself.

"WHO?" Massie asked. "Well, find out. . . . Look, I should get back to work, but I'll see you tomorrow. . . . You'll find out, right? . . . 'Kay, bye."

Claire's fists were clenched. So was her stomach. She had a *feeling* Cam liked her after their Halloween party. Now Massie's conversation had confirmed it! But she was desperate for more information.

"Sounds like you and Alicia are friends again," Claire said from behind the couch.

"Not officially," Massie said. "But she's got the best gossip and I kinda need to be tapped in right now, so—"

"Why, is something going on?"

"She wouldn't tell me over the phone." Massie sounded irritated. "I'll get it out of her tomorrow."

"Oh." Claire hoped Massie wouldn't pick up on her disappointment. "Good luck. Keep me posted."

Massie responded with a yawn. "Look, I'm going to bed. I'm beat."

"Are you finished already?" Claire looked at the mess of needles, thread, and scraps of material around her. She'd need the entire rest of the week to finish! She started to feel panic rising in her chest. Why was she even bothering with this in the first place? She didn't stand a chance.

"No, I still have some finishing touches to put on everything, but I'll do it tomorrow after school. Meet me here, 'kay?" Massie asked.

"Yeah, I'll see you after school," Claire said with a smile, and suddenly realized the reason she was "bothering." For some reason, Massie didn't mind having Claire around while they were working. And Claire wasn't about to give that up. She didn't even care why the change of heart occurred; she was just grateful it had.

"I'm going to pack my stuff up in a garbage bag and leave it by the door and I suggest you do the same." Massie started folding up scraps of unused material. "Unless, of course, you *want* me to peek at your uniform in the middle of the night."

"No way. Give me one of those bags."

Claire didn't actually care if Massie looked at her sample. In fact, she would have been glad. It was the first thing she had ever sewn by herself and she thought she had done a pretty good job. But Massie wanted it that way, so Claire left her bag by the door and turned off the light.

Claire ran all the way back to the guesthouse. Not because she thought psychos were chasing her, like she usually did, but because Massie was finally being nice to her and Cam had a secret crush. Claire just *knew* she was the girl he liked. And all of that made her feel like running.

OCTAVIAN COUNTRY DAY SCHOOL
THE HALLS
11:15 AM
November 4th

Massie raced through the halls, past the Models Wanted signs and the high-gloss Fashion Week at OCD posters. Someone had taken a deep red lipstick and changed a few of them to Fashion WEAK at OCD. But Massie had no time to appreciate the "clever" work of activists. She was in a hurry to find Alicia, who for some reason was not answering her phone.

Massie picked up her pace and raced even faster. All she had to do was confirm that Cam liked her as more than a friend so she could finally start getting some of that valuable "experience with boys" Alicia had been bragging about lately. But Alicia was nowhere to be found.

After ten frantic minutes Massie decided to put her search on hold. She didn't want to be late for the FIT (Fashion Inspiration Trip) of the day or she would miss the chance to see Cynthia Rowley's design studio. Massie ran outside to the parking lot and charged onto the bus. It smelled like leftover tuna sandwiches.

Massie quickly made her way toward Kristen.

Her old denim skirt had bunched up around her legs and she quickly straightened it out when no one was looking. The suede pocket she had sewn on that morning was holding up nicely. She got six compliments on it. She'd even made up a few fake Web site names when people asked where she bought it. Only *she* knew the pockets were pieces of the skirt Todd soaked with grape juice.

"Kristen," Massie panted. "Do you know where Alicia is? She's not answering her phone."

"No." Kristen checked her Coach watch, just like she always did when she was asked a question she couldn't answer. "I don't think she's back from the sample sale yet."

"Didn't she go at like eight in the morning?"

"Yeah, but Olivia wasn't in math, so I guess they're still in the city, looking for uniform ideas," Kristen said.

"She went into the city with *Olivia?*" Massie asked.

"Yeah, I thought you knew that."

Massie shook her head.

Everything around her felt still and a rush of heat burst through her body like fireworks exploding. She usually knew where Alicia was at all times. Now the only thing she knew was that she didn't know anything.

Even though her ears were ringing, Massie heard a frantic voice say, "Has anyone seen Massie Block?" The voice sounded really upset. "It's an emergency."

Massie could not believe that she was seconds away from dealing with an "emergency."

"This year sucks," she said to Kristen.

"Yeah, well, it's about to get worse," Kristen said. "Look who it is."

"You're not going to believe this." Claire stopped in front of Massie's seat. She didn't seem to mind that everyone was waiting for her to get off the bus so they could leave.

"What?" Massie rolled her eyes and tried to look bored. She stole a quick glance at herself in the rearview mirror. She looked good and was glad she had applied a fresh coat of gloss before she got there.

"Our uniforms are gone!" Claire cried. A bubble of saliva formed between her lips when she spoke.

"What do you mean, *gone?*" Massie pulled Claire into an empty seat so they could have some privacy.

"IwantedtoshowmyuniformtomymomthismorningsoIwenttogetmytrashbagand—"

"Slow down," Massie snapped. "I can't understand you."

"Inez threw them out! She thought they were trash."

"What? NO! Why?"

"'Cause they were in trash bags!" Claire shouted. "Remember, you didn't trust me. You thought I would peek at your masterpiece. Well, now your masterpiece is probably on its way to a furnace to in Peekskill burn up."

Massie caught herself wondering how Claire, a girl from Orlando, knew that trash in Westchester went to a furnace in Peekskill, but she was too upset to ask.

Her chance to become famous for leading a style revolution at OCD was gone.

Massie suddenly felt sorry for the white tennis skirt she spent half the night sewing. It was probably in the back of a smelly trash truck buried in rotten eggs and poo-covered diapers, wondering how it got there. The more she thought about it, the more Massie felt sad for everyone: her mother, who took her shopping after school for the material; her proud father, who couldn't wait to see his daughter's masterpiece; Bean, who sacrificed her nightly walk; and even her mannequin, which stood by her all night while she worked. She considered feeling sorry for Claire, but there just wasn't room. She was full.

Claire sniffed and wiped her palm across her moist nose. "It was the first thing I ever made. And it was pretty good."

"Well, I was on my way to making history," Massie said, as if her loss was ten times bigger than Claire's.

"You sew pretty fast," Claire said. "You could probably get something together by Saturday night."

"That's in four days! Do I *look* like I'm from Moscow?"

"No."

"Then why do you think I'd be into Russian?"

Claire laughed. Massie smiled back. She had tried the joke before on Dylan and Kristen and they didn't get it.

"Maybe if we do it together, we could—"

"Not a chance," Massie interrupted. "I want to go down in history alone."

"Hmmm," Claire said.

"What?" Massie gathered her hair in a ponytail and then let it drop back to her shoulders.

"I was just thinking. Nah, forget it. You'd never go for it."

"WHAT?" Massie snapped.

"Wouldn't you love to stand onstage in front of the *Teen People* editors in a brand-new outfit when you present the school with your, I mean *our,* new creation?"

"*Kuh-laire,* I am so not doing this with—" Massie paused. She leaned closer and whispered, "Are you saying you'll call off the bet if I let you partner with me?"

Just then Massie noticed Claire was a full inch taller than she was. She looked down at her feet and noticed the girl was wearing a pair of high-heeled black Capezio dance shoes with *white sweat socks.* At that moment Massie actually found herself missing the Keds.

"Yup," Claire said. "The bet will be over." She shifted her weight from her left foot to her right. "But you'd have to *really* partner with me this time. Not like you did for the Halloween party. This time you have to *mean* it."

"Hmmm." Massie tapped her French-manicured fingernail against her bottom lip. "Let. Me. See."

Claire let out an impatient sigh.

"'Kay, I'll do it!"

Claire's face lit up.

"But I'm only doing this for fashion," Massie added. "And for our mothers, of course."

"Really?" Claire turned on her high heels and made her way toward the front of the bus. "'Cause I'm doing it to win."

Claire pushed her way through the aisle and bounced down the steps of the bus. She ran all the way back to class on her tiptoes to keep from spraining her ankle. Her blond hair whipped across her face, but she never stopped to fix or tie it back. She didn't seem to care.

Massie watched Claire at that moment as if it were the first time she had ever seen her. And in a way, it was.

THE BLOCK ESTATE

FRONT LAWN

3:58 PM

November 6th

Todd Lyons bolted off the Briarwood Academy bus in a flurry of flying juice boxes. He picked one up off the ground and whipped it back on the bus before the driver could get the door closed.

"That's for you, Dick," Todd said. He was doubled over, laughing.

"My name is Richard!"

Massie watched the bus pull away from behind a thick oak on her front lawn. She had been walking Bean and was in no mood to see Todd. She'd taken cover behind the tree and decided to wait there until he was inside the house.

He walked up the driveway, kicking the white stones beneath his feet with every step. The sound made Bean jumpy.

"Shhh." She covered the dog's mouth with her hand.

Todd was almost at the house when the bus pulled up again. It hissed when it stopped and screeched when the doors opened. Someone was getting off.

"Hey, Todd, wait up."

Massie poked her head out from the side of the tree to see who it was.

"TODD!"

"Cam?" Massie said to Bean. "EhmaGOD."

Cam ran up the driveway toward Todd and the two stopped and talked. Massie darted behind another tree, hoping to get closer so she could hear what they were saying. There was enough grass between her and Cam to do at least twenty cartwheels. She couldn't make out a single word. She couldn't smell his Drakkar Noir, couldn't look into his blue or green eye, and couldn't tell what kind of sweater he was wearing under his leather jacket. All she knew for sure was that his skinny butt looked *ah-dorable* in his dark wash Diesel jeans.

She watched Cam tilt his shoulder so his green canvas messenger bag could slide off and fall to the ground. He dropped into a squat and fished around inside until he found what he was looking for: a CD-shaped case wrapped in what looked like a bunch of rubber bands. He pulled it out and handed it to Todd, who put it in his knapsack immediately.

Cam gave Todd two friendly slaps on the shoulder and ran toward the street. Todd stood and waved goodbye, looking just as smitten as Massie did.

She waited until Cam was halfway down the block before she jumped out from behind the tree. "Todd," Massie shouted. "How was your day?"

"It just got better, my pet," he said. "How was yours?"

"Wasn't that Cam Fisher?" Massie quickly glanced at Todd's knapsack, hoping to get a look inside, but it was zipped up.

"Yeah." Todd started walking toward the guesthouse and Massie followed.

"Why was *he* here?" Massie thought if she sounded annoyed, Todd wouldn't pick up on her crush.

"No reason," Todd said. "Hey, wanna come over and play Tony Hawk's Underground?"

"I would love to, but I have to give Bean a bath." Massie put the dog on the ground and fanned the air. "It's been a while and she's starting to smell like feet."

"Let me help." Todd reached down to pat Bean, but the dog ran and hid behind Massie's legs.

Massie couldn't play this game for one more second. She knew Cam had dropped something off for her and she wanted it. Todd was probably holding Cam's love gift hostage because he was jealous.

"Todd, darling." Massie put her hand on his shoulder and they stopped walking. She glared at him with her amber eyes until a bead of sweat formed above his upper lip. "I know what's in the bag and I want it."

"What?" Todd grabbed onto the straps of his backpack with both hands.

"Just give it to me," Massie said.

"You want it?" Todd asked.

"Yes."

"Really?"

"YES!"

"Ohh-kayyy." He slid the bag off his shoulders and stepped closer to Massie.

She could feel her hands getting clammy.

"Ready?" Todd asked.

"READY!" she said.

Todd stood on his toes, sprang forward, and planted his lips right on Massie's.

"Eeewww!" she screamed.

Bean barked.

Massie wiped her mouth with the sleeve of her gold satin bomber jacket. She held Bean and watched the bratty ten-year-old get away.

"Get back here," Massie shouted.

"You want *more?*" He looked back at Massie and winked.

"No, I want what Cam gave you," Massie said.

"Medal of Honor?" Todd asked. "Since when are you into video games?"

"Cam gave you a *video game?*" Massie didn't believe him.

"Yup, I gotta go. I'll call you later." Todd waved. "We'll pick up where we left off."

"Don't count on it."

Seconds later he was gone. And he made off with a lot more than Cam's gift. Because on November 6, at exactly 4:17 PM, Todd Lyons had stolen Massie Block's first kiss. And unfortunately, she'd never get it back.

The Westchester Mall
Level 1
5:17 PM
November 7th

The waxy rope handles on the shopping bags were digging into Massie's hands, yet she found the pain exhilarating. The reddish purple grooves in the middle of her palms were like hard-earned badges of honor, proof of a shopping mission accomplished, a reminder that she was back on the scene after a grueling fifteen-day ban.

Alicia, Kristen, and Dylan had their arms full of an overwhelming amount of Coach, Lacoste, and Guess? bags, but Massie still had more.

"I wish they had shopping carts at malls," Dylan whined. "Think of how much more we could buy if we didn't have to carry it all."

"We should hire a shopping Sherpa." Massie put her foot on a bench and rested her bags on her knee. "You know, some strong little guy that would follow us around all day while we shopped so he could carry everything we bought."

"That's a boyfriend," Alicia said. "And I'm working on it."

Everyone giggled, but Massie cracked up. She had missed Alicia's playful divalike attitude and was overjoyed that for the moment Leesh was Olivia-free and back where she belonged.

"Where is Olivia tonight?" Massie asked, trying to sound genuinely interested.

"She has dance on Fridays," Alicia said.

"And she *went?* The night before the fashion show? Gawd, you must be pissed. I'm sure you wanted to rehearse, right?"

"No, it's fine. She's sleeping over," Alicia said.

"Oh." Massie didn't know where to look.

"Can we go into A&F?" Kristen sped up and led the way.

"You're not going to find anything in Abercrombie that's cute enough to wear to the contest tomorrow night," Alicia said.

"I know, but I need their latest shopping bag for my bedroom wall." Kristen pointed to the poster of the chiseled half-man, half-airbrushed model in the store window and cooed, "And *he* better be on it."

"So you're not sleeping at my place tonight?" Massie asked Alicia. She was sifting through the racks of wool cardigans and denim jackets, trying to sound casual.

"I totally forgot it's Friday," Alicia said. She completely managed to avoid Massie's eyes. She turned toward Kristen and Dylan, who were standing on opposite sides of the T-shirt display table. "Are you guys going?"

"Given," Dylan said.

Kristen nodded.

"Don't you have to finish your uniforms?" Alicia asked.

"We were going to finish them at Massie's," Kristen said.

Alicia slid a bunch of hangers back and forth on the rack.

"Kristen, I thought you were going to practice your soccer kicks with Derrington tonight," Alicia said.

"No, on Monday." Kristen frowned. "What's with the

advertisement?" She stole a glance at Dylan, who turned red with anger, then green with jealousy. Her face matched her hair.

"You're playing soccer with Derrington on Monday?" Dylan unfolded a T-shirt and held it in front of her as if she were checking the size but then threw it on the table without ever looking at it.

"Yeah, I told him I'd take him to a major league soccer game when the season starts if he helps me practice my kicks."

"Sounds more like you're trying to score," Dylan said.

Their constant fighting was starting to bore Massie to tears. At least if they'd been in Louis Vuitton or Sephora, Massie could wander off and shop, but Abercrombie? Ugh! The only fashionable thing in the entire store was *her.*

"I'm sure he'll tell me all about it on our long drive into the city next Wednesday night," Dylan said.

"What do you mean?" Kristen asked. "You're not really going to the city with Derrington on a school night. Are you?"

"Yup. It's Tommy Hilfiger's birthday party at the Four Seasons. My mom and my sisters are all bringing dates, so I invited Derrington and he said yes," Dylan said. "That reminds me, I should buy him a pair of long pants while we're here."

"Sounds to me like he's using both of you." Massie ran her fingers across a pair of baggy cargos. "Ew! This place is so Gap. Now, can we get out of here before I start thinking these clothes are actually cute?"

"Wait, Massie, what do you mean, *using* us?" Dylan said.

"She's right," Alicia jumped in. "He's getting more stuff

than a kid whose parents just got divorced. Kristen, you've practically done all of his homework for the last week, and Dylan, you've been giving him all of the DVDs and video games your mom brings home from work. What has he done for you?"

"Well, he's not using *me!*" Kristen stormed off toward the back of the store.

"Great, now I'll never get out of here." Massie lifted a white lace cami off the shelf. "I might as well try this on."

Alicia yanked a denim mini off a hanger and followed Massie to the dressing rooms.

Kristen was sifting through the sale rack but slowed down when she came to the pleated cord mini in chocolate brown.

"How cute is this?" Kristen said. "And it's on sale!"

"No, it's not." Dylan was standing in front of Kristen, holding the same skirt. "Someone must have hung it there by mistake, because there's a bunch of them at the front of the store."

Kristen looked at the skirt in Dylan's hand, then straight into her green eyes. "You're not getting it, are you?"

"I'm seriously considering it," Dylan said.

"Well, I'm wearing it to the fashion show tomorrow night."

"No, you're not—I am," Dylan said.

Massie walked out of the changing room in a huff and buried the unwanted white cami under a stack of fleece pants.

"I have an idea. One of you can have the skirt and the other can have Derrington," Massie said. "Now can we leave?

I want to get to Versace Jeans before the mall closes."

"While we're on the subject, Kristen copied my idea to design reversible uniforms," Dylan said. "How will you decide who gets that one?"

"Puh-lease," Kristen said. "It wasn't *your* idea, and by the way, your mother's wardrobe stylist is making your entry and we all know it."

"That's cheating! You can't hire a professional," Alicia said as she came out of the changing room. She handed the denim skirt and her credit card to the first salesperson who strolled by. "Can you ring this up? I'll wait here."

The salesgirl snatched the card out of Alicia's hand and swished away in a huff.

"If you ask me, neither of you should get that idea," Massie said.

"Why?" Kristen and Dylan asked at the same time.

"Because it's stupid and if one of you wins, I'll have to spend the rest of my life in a reversible uniform."

The salesgirl returned with Alicia's credit card and her skirt. "Sign here, please, Mr. Antonio Rivera," she said with a grimace.

"Finally." Massie sighed. "I have an idea." Massie was looking at the silk tops but speaking to Kristen and Dylan. "Why don't you guys call it quits on the whole reversible uniform thing and come model for me."

"Fine with me," Kristen said. "I sewed the skirt to my pajama bottoms last night by mistake. At least this way I have a chance to be on a winning team."

"So why don't you do that and I'll take Derrington?" Dylan said.

"OH MY GOD!" Alicia said. "Will you get over him? He's using you guys."

"He may be using Kristen, but he likes me," Dylan said.

"He's using *both* of you. I'll prove it." Alicia plopped herself down on the white leather couch in front of the changing rooms and pulled out her cell phone. "Come sit down."

Kristen and Dylan did as they were told and sat on either side of Alicia.

"Talk loud." Massie's arms were filled with clothes and she headed into the dressing room. "I don't want to miss this."

"Watch," Alicia said. "Kris, you have plans with him on Monday, right?"

"Yup."

Alicia sat forward and sent Derrington a message on her phone. The girls crowded around her, trying to see what she was doing.

ALICIA: ? R U DOING MONDAY AFTER SCHOOL?
DERRICK: PLAYING SOCCER. Y?

Kristen beamed with pride when she saw his response. "Seeee," she said.

ALICIA: PARENTS R AWAY.
DERRICK: COOL.
ALICIA: WANTED 2 HAVE HOT TUB PARTY.

DERRICK: WHO'S GOING?
ALICIA: ME ☺
DERRICK: TIME?

"What time are you supposed to play soccer?" Alicia asked Kristen.

"Four thirty," Kristen said. Her smile faded.

ALICIA: 4:30
DERRICK: I'LL B THERE.

"Looks like we have our answer." Dylan dabbed on a bit of lip gloss. "He obviously doesn't like you very much."

Alicia turned to face Dylan. "What time are you supposed to meet him on Wednesday?"

"Six," Dylan said. "Why?"

But Alicia didn't answer.

ALICIA: SORRY, MADE A MISTAKE. HOT TUB ON WEDNESDAY AT SIX. STILL COOL?
DERRICK: WOULDN'T MISS IT.

"And that, my friends, is what you call a dirtbag." Alicia dropped her phone into her Prada and got up to check on Massie's progress. "You can take the guy out of the Halloween costume, but you can't take the Halloween costume out of the guy."

Massie hurried out of the dressing room. She didn't want to miss Dylan and Kristen's reactions.

The girls were silent. They couldn't even bring themselves to look at each other. Kristen crossed and uncrossed her legs and Dylan helped herself to a handful of mints from the silver dish on the magazine table that was in front of them.

"I can't believe him," Dylan said. "He was so excited to go into the city with me."

"Yeah, about as excited as he was to play soccer with me," Kristen said.

Dylan grabbed another handful of mints and slid the dish toward Kristen. She shook her head no and smiled thanks.

"I'm such an idiot," Dylan said.

"For thinking Derrington would like you?" Kristen said.

"NO!" Dylan snapped. "For letting him come between us."

"I know." Kristen uncrossed her legs and turned to face Dylan. "We have to get back at him."

"Yeah," Dylan agreed. She slapped her hand against her heart and closed her eyes, slowly shaking her head. "What were we thinking?"

"We weren't."

"Hug?"

"Hug."

The girls hugged and vowed never to let a guy come between them again, especially a horn dog like Derrington.

"Does this mean you two will join my team and be my models?" Massie asked. She had jeans in every wash hanging over her shoulders and bright-colored tops draped across her arms. "We can rehearse tonight."

"Does this mean we have to be nice to Claire?" Kristen asked.

"I hope not," Dylan said. "I'm still mad at her for IM'ing us from Massie's computer." She turned toward Massie. "She totally had me convinced that you thought I was fat."

"And that you wanted us to wear jean shorts and tights to school," Alicia said.

"I still can't believe you thought I would actually send IMs like that," Massie said.

"So then why do we have to be nice to her?" Dylan said.

"Because she'll thread all of our needles since she doesn't have any nails," Massie said. "So try not to piss her off or *we'll* have to do it."

"Done."

"Done."

Massie was waiting for Alicia to say "and done" but then remembered she wasn't part of their team.

"By the way, Alicia, can I have your bag?" Kristen was staring at the black-and-white Abercrombie model that was swinging back and forth in Alicia's hand.

"Sure, you can have the skirt too if you want," Alicia said, handing it over. "I don't really like it."

They waited by the doors near Neiman's for Massie's driver to pick them up. As always, Isaac pulled up in the Range Rover exactly on time.

They spent the ride singing to the radio and gossiping about the annoying girls in their grade, just like they always did. But something felt different. It was the first Friday night in over a year that Alicia wasn't sleeping over at Massie's.

They pulled up to the black iron gates in front of Alicia's house and Isaac helped her gather her bags.

"Have fun at the sleepover. I'll miss you guys," Alicia said as she backed out of the SUV. "I hate that I have to compete against my best friends in the entire world. This whole thing sucks." She contorted her face into a pouty frown.

But Massie wasn't buying it. Alicia's brown eyes sparkled and danced a little too much for someone as tortured as she had just claimed to be.

OCTAVIAN COUNTRY DAY SCHOOL
SAGAMORE HALL
6:45 PM
November 8th

Backstage, the models were panicking. Some had stage fright. Others simply refused to put on their uniforms because they thought they looked fat or they didn't want to change in front of Eli.

Claire stood by the refreshments table and licked chocolate icing off her fingers.

Massie came over to grab a bottle of Smart Water.

"Well, this is it," Massie said. She looked incredible. Her straight hair was loose and wavy and she looked like a French model in her new outfit, a frilly see-through cap-sleeved shirt with a beige cami underneath and a peach skirt that swished and swayed when she walked. And she was already wearing the black beret they'd promised to save for the show.

Claire saw that exact outfit in *Teen Vogue* when she was researching design ideas. The skirt alone cost $350.

"You look really good," Claire said. She looked down at her new red moccasins and wished her mom had let her buy something with a low heel instead.

"Thanks," Massie said. "What happened to your hand?"

"Doughnuts." Claire looked embarrassed.

"No, the Band-Aids." Massie adjusted her beret to give it more of a tilt.

"Oh, I got a few blisters from threading all those needles last night. But it's no big deal. I had fun," Claire said. "Especially when we did the fashion shoot. I can't wait to e-mail those pictures to my friends back home."

"Yeah, it was fun." Massie sounded surprised. "I can't believe we stayed up until four o'clock in the morning. Thank *Gawd* for espresso machines."

"And Dylan's farts," Claire said. "They kept me alert for hours."

Massie cracked up. Claire laughed too, then rubbed her tired, burning eyes. She felt better than she had in a long time.

"Well, at least they finally forgave me for sending those IMs," Claire said.

"Yeah, and *all* you had to do was sew their uniforms and make them popcorn while they watched E! for three hours straight," Massie said.

"It was worth it."

"What are you *doing* here?"

Claire turned to see one of Pia's butt-kissing teacher's assistants approaching. She held a clipboard and had a walkie-talkie clipped to the side of her Sevens. "Why aren't you in hair and makeup?"

"We're not models," Massie said. "We just happen to look *ah-mazing.*"

"Well, it says right here that you both signed up for model's robes." She flipped through the pages on her clipboard.

"We don't want people to see what we're going to be wearing," Massie said back.

"But you're just presenting." The assistant sounded confused.

"That's what you think," Claire said.

Claire and Massie rehearsed their lines one last time, checked in on Kristen and Dylan in the makeup chairs, and then snuck over to the curtain to peek out at the audience.

The DJ was already blasting music to the house. The show was still fifteen minutes away and the seats were already full.

"Opening night of *The Producers* on Broadway didn't look half this packed," Massie whispered to Claire, their heads poking through the red velvet curtain. "Look—there are the editors from *Teen People*. Front row center."

"God, there are so many photographers." Claire bit down on her thumbnail.

As impressed as she was by the turnout, Claire really only cared about seeing one person. She searched the audience, looking for the mess of black hair, the slouchy posture, and the brown leather jacket.

"Girls, you should be with your models," Principal Burns cawed.

Claire had never seen Burns at such close range before. With her pointy hook nose and her tiny eyes she really *did* look like a buzzard.

"The show is about to start and I need you in your places," she said. "Now, fly!"

The girls giggled all the way to their places. They couldn't believe the bird lady actually told them to "fly."

Everyone was lined up according to the order of their appearance onstage. Massie, Dylan, Kristen, and Claire were last.

"I hope people don't fall asleep before our turn," Dylan whispered.

The hairstylist had glossed each one of her red ringlets individually so they glistened and bounced. Her already piercing green eyes had gotten the smoky treatment from the Bobbi Brown makeup artist. They were glowing.

"Trust me, we're in the best position," Massie said. "Right after we go, the audience votes. So if we make it into the finals, we'll be fresh in their minds."

"Wow, we got lucky," Claire said.

"No, we didn't," Massie said. "I called Pia last night and asked for this spot."

"And she just gave it to you?" Kristen kept her neck perfectly still as she talked to keep the tower of blond hair on her head from collapsing.

"Don't forget, this whole contest was *my* idea," Massie said. "It was the least she could do."

The music stopped and the houselights fell. The room was surprisingly quiet except for the sounds of people shifting in their seats and folding their programs while they got comfortable. But as soon as Principal Burns took the mike, they exploded with applause. The sound made Claire think of frying bacon.

The pink lights from the runway seeped through the cracks of the curtains and cast bars of color across the girls in the wings. Claire scanned the line, stealing glances at her competition.

Layne and Eli were standing beside each other, swaying back and forth, letting their shoulders gently collide over and over again to an inaudible rhythm that must have been playing inside their heads. Claire couldn't wait to brush shoulders with someone of her own and immediately thought of Cam.

"Good luck," Layne whispered to Claire when she caught her staring.

"You too," Claire mouthed back. She meant it. She had missed Layne over the last few days and couldn't wait for Fashion Week to be over so things could go back to normal. Even if it meant wearing something Eli was about to model.

Alicia and Olivia oozed confidence. Olivia's new nose was powdered to perfection and her blond hair was blown stick straight. It touched the small of her back. Her sky blue eyes were surrounded by black liner, which somehow made them look more piercing and focused. And Alicia was the exact opposite. Her dark, rich features looked soft and warm in comparison but equally as powerful. She was even more beautiful than Olivia but in a less obvious way.

Claire watched Kristen and Dylan fussing with each other's hair, fighting gravity to make sure every silky strand was in its proper place. *We're going to lose,* she thought.

"Welcome to OCD's Fashion Week," Principal Burns announced. "On behalf of the students who have worked very hard this week, I would like to thank you all for coming."

Applause.

"Before . . . ," she continued, but was forced to wait another second for the applause to die down completely. "Before we get started, I would like to—"

"Awww, awww," someone shouted from the audience. The heckler was doing his best buzzard imitation.

After a series of short giggles and several terse "shhh's," Principal Burns picked up where she left off.

"I would like to thank the editors of *Teen People* for being here tonight. As you know, they will narrow the contestants down to two finalists and then turn the voting over to you, the students of OCD, because you put the *u* in *uniform.*"

Roaring applause.

"We . . ." She paused to throw in a humble chuckle and raised her hand for silence. "We have a professional photographer here to document tonight's show, and with a twenty-dollar donation—"

"Awww, awww."

Half the audience giggled and the other half shifted nervously in their seats.

She waited.

"I suppose we should just get started. Please turn your cell phones off—"

Claire heard more giggling, but this time it came from Kristen and Dylan.

"What?" Claire mouthed.

"You'll see," they mouthed back, and smiled.

Claire's entire body started beating wildly, and suddenly something felt very wrong.

I knew I shouldn't have trusted them.

Now that Claire was in danger, the festive atmosphere suddenly felt threatening. The pretty girls looked like clowns in their makeup, the applause sounded like gunfire, and the uniforms looked like they were made by blind kids with no hands. The love was gone.

Claire tried to calm down by focusing on the show.

Ann Marie Blanc was the first to present. She proposed the students wear cashmere sweater sets and taffeta skirts.

"Next." Massie folded her arms and rolled her eyes. "She's done."

"Why?" Claire whispered.

"Taffeta's wrinkle potential is off the charts and we'll *roast* in that cashmere," she said.

"Oh."

Mindee Wilson presented her Days of the Week uniform as her five models pranced around the runway, each wearing an unflattering sack dress in a different color with a different day of the week written across the chest. Monday's dress was red and said Monday across the chest, and Tuesday's dress was blue and said Tuesday across the chest, and . . .

"Cute," Dylan mumbled. "If you're in K through 2."

"Yeah, imagine flirting with a Briarwood boy in a pink sack that said Thursday," Kristen said.

Claire giggled. She thought of Cam.

Livid Altman called her masterpiece Black on Black with a Splash of Black for obvious reasons. She tried to convince the *Teen People* editors that black was the only real option because it hid dirt so well and therefore required less cleaning. But Claire heard the words *funeral, depressing,* and *unhygienic* being uttered among the crowd.

Layne and Eli were next and the audience erupted in a series of supportive "whoo's."

Claire prayed Massie would like Layne's design. She didn't want her friend to be the subject of ridicule.

Layne took her time walking to the microphone. She cleared her throat before she spoke.

"OCD is committing a crime by forcing developing girls to abandon their identities, especially in these formative years," Layne said. Eli pranced around the runway in a navy pleated skirt, black Chuck Taylor high-tops, and a long-sleeve T-shirt with a plastic pocket sewn across the front.

"The *Teen People* editors are probably thinking *N-O,*" Massie said to Claire.

Claire pretended she hadn't heard.

When Eli got to the front of the stage, he stopped and pulled a stack of index cards out of his book bag. He held them up to the crowd like a magician showing off his "perfectly normal pigeon."

"Clothes are my way of showing the world how I feel, and this uniform will let us continue doing that even after the school has completely stripped us of our personal style," Layne said.

That's when Eli slid the cards in the pocket one by one so the audience could read them.

CONFIDENT
CASUAL BUT SEXY
I FEEL FAT TODAY
I JUST BOUGHT THE NEW SEVENS

The crowd laughed.

When Layne's presentation was over, everyone gave her a standing ovation. Even the women from *Teen People* rose out of their chairs. But they sat back down when they noticed Principal Burns and Pia glaring at them.

Alicia and Olivia were next. The sound of boys leaning forward in their seats filled the room when they took the stage. The photographer started snapping away.

Olivia took off her robe. She walked the runway, swinging her arms back and forth like the models on the Style Network. Theirs was the only campaign that proposed strappy sandals, jeans, and a blazer instead of the cliché schoolgirl skirt, and the crowd ate it up. It was the perfect blend of sexy, sophisticated, and whimsical. While Olivia walked, spun, and strutted, Alicia explained that the blazer was a "nod to Ralph Lauren's Blue Label" and that he had agreed to manufacture the entire line for OCD if they won. She held up poster boards that were checked with different-color swatches so the girls could see "the variety of hues that blended" with the tweed blazer, should they decide to wear this "extremely practical piece" after hours. A man's necktie hung casually from Olivia's belt loops and Alicia explained that groups of girls could wear matching ties to show who their friends were.

Principal Burns jumped out of her seat and yelled, "No way!" but the crowd was too fixated on Alicia and Olivia to notice.

"She got the tie-as-belt idea from me," Massie hissed. "I wore it to the mall that day we went costume shopping and she *complimented* me on it."

"Imitation is the sincerest form of flattery," Claire said, trying to sound supportive.

"Yeah, but if that wins this for her, I'll wrap that form of flattery around her neck and strangle her." Massie folded her arms across her chest.

Claire thought it best to leave it at that.

The audience was already on their feet before Alicia and Olivia took their first bows.

Massie clapped and smiled, but she looked hollow, like a wax museum version of herself.

Claire couldn't believe she had to follow two standing ovations. Kristen and Dylan were obviously worried. They were bouncing up and down on their toes as if trying to burn off their nervous energy. Claire was so nervous she couldn't even move. Not only was she about to go onstage, but she also had to prepare herself for the possibility that this might be the moment when Massie, Dylan, and Kristen decide to humiliate her on a grand scale.

The audience sounded more than ready for the intermission. Parents were chasing their little kids up and down the aisles. People were gathering their belongings in anticipation of the coming break. Claire tugged on her in-between-stage bangs, hoping to inspire a major growth spurt before the show. Massie must have sensed Claire's apprehension because she squeezed her arm and said, "Let's crush 'em!" before leading her team onstage.

The four girls stood beside each other, facing the audience. They were still wearing their robes.

"Take it off," someone shouted from the audience.

"Oh, we will," Massie said, putting on her best sultry voice.

When the hollering died down, she began.

"Four girls," she started. "One redhead, one dark blond, one towhead, and one brunette—" Dylan, Kristen, Claire, and Massie slipped out of their robes and let them fall to the ground. The striptease, as G-rated as it was, captured the boys' attention.

Christina Aguilera's "Dirrty" kicked in and the girls separated, each taking a different corner of the runway. The song choice was their secret homage to the costumes that got them there in the first place.

"We invite you to ask yourself," Massie continued,

"'What color palette is right for me?' Is your hair brown or black? And does your skin tone range from ivory to deep brown? If so, then you're a 'Massie' and your uniform should be pure white and green," Claire said. As she spoke, Massie paraded around the runway, making sharp turns and waving to her adoring fans. She wore a dark green suede skirt that was an exact replica of the one Todd had destroyed with grape juice—soft, short, and A-line. It had a purple rhinestone holster clipped to the side for her cell phone. Right when the explosive chorus in the song hit, Massie took off her matching green blazer, complete with a big yellow flower pinned to the lapel, and hung it over her shoulder. The black beret made her look like the charming French model she always knew she could be.

Applause.

A white strapless silk top with the letter *M* stitched in the upper left corner was underneath. Purple-rhinestone-covered platform Keds with black knee-high socks rounded out the look.

Roaring applause.

"Or maybe you're a 'Kristen,'" Claire said, giving Kristen the cue to start walking. "Your hair ranges from brown to blond and your skin has golden tones. Sound familiar? If it does, your uniform will be soft white, red, and turquoise." Kristen wore the same outfit as Massie, only her suede skirt and blazer were red, her flower was turquoise, the rhinestones on her cell phone holder and Keds were white, and the letter on her white sleeveless top was a *K.* She twirled her beret on her finger because it refused to balance on her updo.

Once she completed her lap, Claire handed the microphone to Massie, who continued the presentation.

"Do you burn in the sun and look positively sickly in beige?" Massie asked. "If you do, then you're a 'Claire' and you're all pastels. . . . Hey, someone's gotta wear those Easter egg shades, right?"

The audience laughed.

Claire skipped around the runway, holding her beret in place so it wouldn't slip. She wore a baby blue suede skirt and blazer and a pink flower on her lapel and the letter *C* was stitched on her top. Her black-rhinestone-covered cell phone holder was empty. But for the first time in weeks her Keds were full.

"Fiery redheads, you're a 'Dylan.' Your uniform will be ivory and lavender," Massie said as Dylan walked, "the perfect shades to accentuate your rosy tones.

"And of course, no uniform is complete without a version designed for woman's best friend." Massie blew into the Tiffany whistle that hung from a silver chain around her neck. Right on cue, Bean appeared from the wings of the stage and ran straight for her owner. She wore a green suede skirt and a white T-shirt with a B across the back. A tiny black beret sat between her pointy ears.

The audience was on their feet and Bean barked for joy. Massie, Claire, Dylan, and Kristen joined hands and bowed. They killed!

The bright lights were shining right in Claire's eyes, making it hard for her to spot her parents. But one face in the third row was crystal clear. It was Cam's. He was slouched down in his seat. Claire thought he looked like he was being swallowed by his leather jacket. The instant he locked eyes with her, Claire's heart jumped. He offered up a big smile and a small wave, which made all of the noise in the room sound dull and muted, like her head was in a fishbowl.

Claire raised her hand without lifting her arm and waved, one finger at a time. Cam's face lit up when he saw her wave and she beamed right back at him. She couldn't believe this was happening. She turned to Massie, desperate for a witness, but what she saw made her blood freeze up like dog pee on a cold sidewalk.

There was Massie, amber eyes shining, lip gloss glistening, and brown hair shimmering, waving to Cam.

Claire was mortified.

Cam likes Massie! Not me. How many people saw me wave to him? Did he see? What am I supposed to do with my hands now? THIS SKIRT HAS NO POCKETS!

Claire would have taken public humiliation at the hands of Kristen and Dylan over *this* any day.

Principal Burns reclaimed the stage and called all of the competitors out to join her. They huddled together in tight clusters while they waited for the *Teen People* editors to decide on the finalists.

When Principal Burns had the envelope in her claws, she made the announcement.

"You all received a thimble from our helpful ushers, and you'll need that now for voting. There are two clear boxes in the hall with the pictures of our two finalists on them. Please drop your thimble in the box of the candidate you wish to vote for and we will have your results after intermission," she explained.

"Awww, awww," said the heckler.

Mild laughter.

"And the finalists are . . . Alicia Rivera and Olivia Ryan and Massie Block, Claire Lyons, Dylan Marvil, and Kristen Gregory."

She continued by congratulating all of the other girls on their hard work, but no one was listening. They were already halfway out the door and eager to cast their votes.

OCTAVIAN COUNTRY DAY SCHOOL
SAGAMORE HALL
8:15 PM
November 8th

Massie couldn't believe she was standing with her arms around Claire, Kristen, and Dylan, jumping for joy.

Claire!

One month ago she never would have thought it possible.

"Come on, let's go vote." Massie felt around the inside of Bean's pink Coach doggie bag and pulled out a thimble and her purple nail polish. It was warm because the puppy had been sitting on it.

"What are you gonna do with that?" Claire asked, pointing to the Urban Decay bottle.

"I'm going to paint my thimble purple before I drop it in the box," Massie said. "For good luck."

"Hey, Mass, will you vote for us?" Dylan asked. "Kris and I have a little business to take care of."

The two girls giggled and dropped their thimbles in Massie's palm.

"Sure," Massie said with a knowing smile, "anything to help the cause."

The three girls shared a laugh before Kristen and Dylan turned back toward the empty assembly hall and crept inside.

"Massie, if you guys have another trick planned to embarrass me in front of—," Claire started to say. Massie cut her off before she could finish.

"Claire, do I look like a total female dog?"

"Wait, Massie, I'm not calling you a *total bitch,*" Claire said. "It's just that in the past, you guys have—"

"Fine, I'll admit it." Massie stopped walking so she could paint her thimble. "Dylan and Kristen have something fabulously nasty planned, but believe it or not, it has nothing to do with you."

Claire looked wary.

"Tormenting you is so September." Massie locked eyes with Claire. "It's out."

"Does that mean I'm *in?*" Claire asked. Her blue eyes were wide and full of hope.

But Massie didn't answer. She blew the polish on her thimble and patted it with her index finger to make sure it was dry. "Let's vote."

Alicia and Olivia were already in the crowded lobby, campaigning for votes and complimenting the *Teen People* editors on their outfits.

Massie's first instinct was to campaign harder, but when she saw the number of thimbles in her box, she realized it wasn't necessary. They were leading by at least thirty. Massie kissed her purple thimble and dropped it in along with Kristen's and Dylan's. She looked at the picture that was taped to the side and giggled. She looked normal—gorgeous, in fact—but Claire's eyes were crossed.

On purpose! The photographer had offered to reshoot the picture, but Claire insisted on leaving it. She said it would make people laugh.

Claire spent the rest of the break comforting Layne. Massie went to check in with her competition.

Alicia and Olivia were standing by the voting table.

"You know what's funny about the word *thimble,*" Olivia said between sips of Perrier. She was talking to a boy who was about to cast his vote. "It sounds like I'm trying to say 'symbol,' but I have a lisp." She giggled to herself. "I thined up for band and now I'm thdudying the thimbles. Thounds like I'm lisping, right?"

Massie watched as the boy rolled his eyes. He dropped his thimble into Massie's box.

"Thtupid," Alicia called after the boy. Massie laughed, but Olivia was too upset to join her.

"You know, Massie," Olivia said. "Your team totally has an advantage because you have four people and we only have two, which means you'll get more votes because you have twice as many family members on your side as we do."

"Yeah, but you have a plastic surgeon, a shrink, and three of your father's secret girlfriends, so we're about even." Massie turned on her rubber platforms and left to find her parents.

The lights in the lobby began to flicker and Pia's assistants shepherded people back to their seats.

Once everyone was inside, Principal Burns returned to the podium.

"Can I please have the finalists up here onstage," she said. "Oh, and all cell phones off."

At that exact moment someone in the audience got a call. Their phone's ring tone was set to the tune "Pop Goes the Weasel."

Everyone laughed and searched for the guilty party.

Principal Burns put her hands on her hips and scanned the audience.

"It was him," shouted a young girl with a mousy-colored bob. She pointed to Derrington.

"I swear it wasn't," he shouted. The audience laughed. "I left my phone in my father's Mercedes."

Principal Burns stared him down anyway, for good measure.

"Before we announce tonight's winner, I would like to thank Pia and—"

Doo doo, doo doo, doodoodoodoodoo, doo doo, doo doo, doo doo . . .

Everyone turned to look at Derrington.

"I swear," he said. He put his hand on his heart and laughed nervously.

"Then why are you finding this so amusing?" Principal Burns asked.

"I'm not." He laughed again. His face turned bloodred.

Doo doo, doo doo, doodoodoodoodoo, doo doo, doo doo, doo doo . . .

Finally Principal Burns stepped down from the stage and stormed over to Derrington. She forced him to stand up while she frisked him, which made the whole room erupt.

Derrington shook his head and put his face in his hands while the bird lady plucked at him with her long, bony fingers.

People were clapping, cheering, and "aww-awwing," but no one got more pleasure out of the scene than Kristen and Dylan, who had duct-taped the ringing cell phone to the bottom of Derrington's seat during intermission. They dialed it up one last time just to see what would happen next.

Doo doo, doo doo, doodoodoodoodoo, doo doo, doo doo, doo doo . . .

Principal Burns followed the ring tone to the bottom of his chair and yanked it loose. She held it proudly above her head like it was her first Oscar and the whole room gave her a spirited round of applause. She personally dragged Derrington out of the assembly hall.

"Take over, P," she shouted over her shoulder to Pia.

"Sorry 'bout that," Pia said. She lowered the microphone to her mouth. "Okay, let's bring those boxes out here and announce tonight's winner."

Her assistant struggled as she tried to carry both boxes at the same time, but no one thought to help her. They were all too nervous to think of anyone but themselves.

Pia walked around the box with Massie and Claire's picture on it and then examined the one with Alicia and Olivia's photo. She was obviously doing it for dramatic purposes because everyone knew the thimbles had already been counted backstage.

"I feel like I'm going to barf," Massie said as she squeezed Bean to her chest.

Claire was too busy chewing her fingernails to respond.

"With 102 thimbles, we have Massie and Claire," Pia said.

The two girls started jumping up and down. They reached for Kristen and Dylan, who immediately started bouncing with them.

"And with 136 thimbles, we have Alicia and Olivia. Congratulations, you are the winners of the OCD Fashion Week Uniform Contest. Looks like it's blazers, jeans, and tie belts from here on out!"

Massie stopped bobbing. Alicia started.

"How is that possible?" Massie asked. She immediately thought of Cam and how badly she wanted him to see her win.

"I bet all the boys voted for them." Kristen wiped a tear from her eye.

Claire was just as shocked. "But we had *way* more than them during the break."

Alicia and Olivia were kissing their hands, then waving to the audience.

"Ew," Dylan said. "Could they *be* any more conceited?"

"Did you see my parents jump out of their seats when Pia announced our names?" Kristen wiped another tear away.

"No, but I saw them sit back down again when she announced Alicia and Olivia's," Dylan said.

Kristen's tears came harder and Dylan hugged her.

"Stop or you'll make *me* cry," Claire said.

Dylan and Kristen held out their arms and welcomed Claire into their pity party.

Massie refused to look defeated. Not in front of all these people, and especially not in front of Alicia. Instead she slowly inched her way toward the ballot boxes to take a closer look.

The sound of applause and hip-hop music swirled around inside her head and she had to keep reminding herself that it wasn't for her. Now all she had to look forward to were a bunch of cheesy one-liners like "You're *all* winners" and "You're lucky to have made it that far." Looks of pity from her parents' friends and offers to go for ice cream were minutes away from becoming her reality. It wasn't fair. They worked so hard. TWICE!

"There has to be a mistake," Massie said to herself. She bent down to examine the evidence.

Her own purple thimble was in the box with Alicia and Olivia's picture.

"Look," Massie said as she pointed her discovery out to her teammates.

"Why did you vote for ALICIA?" Dylan snapped.

"I didn't, airhead!" Massie said. "Gawd, don't be such an *Olivia.*"

"They must have switched our pictures," Claire said.

"Ehmagod," Dylan yelped. "You're right."

"Let's tell Pia," Kristen said. "Quick, grab the microphone. Tell everyone." She darted toward the podium.

"No, don't," Massie commanded. "Don't tell anyone about this. Not yet. I need to think."

"But—," Claire said.

"Let's lie still in the weeds like animals do when they're about to kill. Then, when the time is exactly right, we'll pounce."

"Easy, Crocodile Hunter," Dylan said. "You're freaking me out."

"You have to trust me," Massie insisted. "I promise we will make them pay for this. We just have to think of the perfect plan."

"Fine," Kristen said. "But I can't believe we're going to let her get away with it."

"We can always have my mom do a story about this on *The Daily Grind,*" Dylan said. "By Monday afternoon the whole country will know that Alicia and Olivia are criminals."

"Yeah, and I'll have my dad make sure this whole uniform thing never happens. I'll ask him to build a wing here or something," Massie said. "And when the time is right, we'll show everyone who the *real* losers are."

Massie hoped her I've-got-everything-under-control act was convincing because on the inside, she felt ill. Alicia had gone from being her best friend to her biggest enemy in less than five minutes, leaving her too hurt to be angry and too angry to be hurt.

"Hey, Massie, nice going," Alicia said. They were backstage, gathering their belongings. "You totally gave us a run for our money."

Massie had a lump in her stomach and could barely look Alicia in the eye.

"The weeds," she mouthed to the others over her shoulder, but she was also reminding herself.

"I consider this victory a win for all of us," Alicia said. "I mean, we're still best friends, right?"

"Of course, we couldn't be happier for you," Massie said through her teeth.

"By the way, I have some gossip," Alicia said. "But I won't ask for points. Consider this one a gift." She was twirling a ruby-and-gold ring on her index finger.

"Uh-huh." Massie sounded bored.

"Someone likes you," Alicia gushed. "A lot."

"Really?" Massie asked. "Who?" She tried to sound uninterested, but her insides were thumping and pounding. Cam liked her. Cam, with the green and blue eyes, liked her. Not Alicia, not Olivia, not Dylan, not Kristen, not some eighth grader, but her. The night was almost good again.

"Derrington," Alicia said.

"What about him?" Massie asked.

"He *likes* you. He told me himself. But he begged me not to tell you, so don't tell anyone, 'kay?"

"Really?" Massie crinkled her eyebrows. "Are you sure?"

"Yeah," Alicia said. "My gossip is always right. Why?"

"For some reason, I thought you were going to say Cam," Massie said nonchalantly.

"No, he likes someone else, but he still won't say who it is," Alicia said.

Massie looked at the rhinestone-covered Keds on her feet. Nothing made sense.

"So what are you going to do about Kristen and Dylan?"

Massie's brain was reeling and she suddenly felt very thirsty.

"Wouldn't he rather like Kristen or Dylan?" Massie asked.

"He told me he only made plans with *them* 'cause he thought you'd be there." Alicia seemed thrilled by this news, but Massie couldn't understand why. "So what are you going to do?"

"I'm going to go find my parents and maybe grab some ice cream," Massie said. She walked away from Alicia in a daze.

If Cam didn't like *her,* then who *did* he like? She was too overwhelmed to get to the bottom of it tonight, but tomorrow she would launch a full investigation. And when she found out, she would fight that girl to the finish.

FRANKIE'S BISTRO

UPSTAIRS DINING ROOM

9:30 PM

November 8th

Todd stood up and raised his virgin colada high in the air.

"I'd like to make a toast," he said as he tapped a fork against the side of his glass. "To the greatest designers on the planet . . ."

"To the greatest designers on the planet," the Blocks and the Lyonses repeated, looking at the two girls at the end of the table.

"Abercrombie and Fitch," Todd said.

Todd was pelted with a few half-eaten dinner rolls and dirty napkins. The parents never would have allowed that if they hadn't been in the restaurant's private upstairs dinning room.

"No, really," he said. "Even though I voted for Alicia, I think you guys did an amazing job tonight."

A butter packet hit the side of his head, courtesy of Massie.

"I love it when you get angry, my pet," he said.

Jay and Judi Lyons rolled their eyes at their son's behavior as they tried to keep themselves from laughing.

"'Kay, I'm being serious now." Todd reached under the table and pulled out three lilacs for Massie. "They're purple, your favorite color."

A round of gasps and "ahhh's" were heard from the parents.

"That's very sweet, Todd, but I will never, ever, ever, ever be your girlfriend," Massie said as she sniffed the flowers.

"Never say never, ever, ever, ever," Todd said with a suave wink. He puckered his lips.

Massie winced and wiped her mouth with her wrist.

"And Claire, my darling sister, I wrote you this note just to let you know how proud I am of you."

Claire eyed the folded envelope in his clammy hand. She took it slowly and cautiously as if she were expecting it to explode in her face. She ran her pinky finger along the flap and tore it open, never once taking her suspicious eyes off her brother.

"Should I read it out loud?" Claire asked.

"It's a little emotional. Maybe you should take it to the bathroom," Todd suggested.

Claire knew something was up. She had only seen her brother get emotional once, when Nathan beat him at his brand new Formula 1 video game.

"Okay," Claire said as she pushed her chair away from the table and stood up. "Mom, will you order me a fudge sundae?"

Once Claire was in the bathroom, she took the letter out of the envelope and started reading. After the first sentence she lifted her head and looked around for hidden cameras.

"This has to be a joke," she said to the bathroom attendant.

"'Scuse me, honey?"

"Nothing," Claire said. She locked herself in a stall so she could have a little privacy.

DEAR CLAIRE,

YOU MUST HAVE REALLY HATED THE CD I MADE YOU CUZ YOU NEVER GOT BACK TO ME ABOUT THE MOVIE. ANYWAY, I THOUGHT YOUR UNIFORM WAS AWESOME AND I THINK YOU SHOULD HAVE WON.

—CAM

P.S. THE KEDS WERE A COOL TOUCH.

Claire read the note four more times before she left the stall. She had so many questions, but the first one was for Todd.

She hugged her brother to thank him for his "sweet note," and when she was close to his ear, she whispered, "How did you get this?"

"He gave it to me to give to you," Todd said quietly.

"Why did you say you wrote it?" Claire asked, still holding him close.

"Cuz I got Massie flowers and I didn't have anything for you. I felt guilty."

Claire hugged her brother again.

"Do you know anything about a CD?" Claire asked.

"Uh, yeah," Todd said. "I've been meaning to give it to you. It's killer."

Claire would have punched him, but she was much too happy.

The waiter came with a cart filled with desserts: pies, cakes, cookies, flans, and tarts. Mr. Block asked for one of everything because they were celebrating.

“What could we possibly be celebrating, Dad?” Massie asked. She stuffed a spoonful of butterscotch ice cream in her mouth.

“That you don’t have to wear that horrible sweater set Ann Marie Blanc came up with,” he said.

Everyone laughed and praised the fashion gods for small miracles.

“Yeah, but now we have to wear strappy sandals,” Claire said.

“Not if my smart, brilliant, powerful, handsome father donates a building or something to the fashion department so we can wear what we want again.” Massie batted her eyelashes and tossed in a few “pretty please’s” for effect.

Claire saw Mr. Block’s face soften and decided to join in.

“Oh, please, William. Pleeease.”

“Look who has suddenly taken an interest in fashion,” Judi Lyons said to her daughter.

“Would you be begging William to fix things if you girls won tonight?” Claire’s father asked.

“We did win and I’m still—”

Claire felt the pointy toe of Massie’s boot jab her shin.

"Ouch," Claire said.

"Weeds," Massie mouthed.

Claire looked at her with a sincere apology in her eyes and Massie smiled.

"What do you mean, you won?" Jay asked.

"Well, not literally, Dad," Claire said. "I mean I won because I had a good time."

Claire got another kick under the table, but this one was softer. Massie made a face like she was trying to suppress her giggles. Claire knew she had done well.

"When did you change out of your Keds?" Claire whispered. She was rubbing her leg under the table.

"Immediately after the show," Massie said.

They laughed.

For that one moment Claire stopped being afraid of Massie. The girl with the amber eyes was no longer a mysterious she-devil. She stressed over outfits, got stabbed in the back by her friends, liked sugary desserts, and didn't always win, even when she deserved to. Massie was a regular person. She just knew how to hide it.

Claire watched Massie wipe the sides of her mouth with a cloth napkin and reapply a fresh coat of lip gloss. And she began to understand why Massie waited so long to accept her.

Like the right to wear a Dirty Devil costume, Massie's friendship wasn't something Claire was entitled to: it was something she had earn. And she had finally done it.

Claire slid her hand into the back pocket of her Gap

jeans and touched the folded note from Cam to make sure it was still there.

I'll show it to Massie after dinner, she thought. Claire couldn't wait to see her reaction. She imagined they would hug, jump up and down, and read it over and over again until they knew every word by heart. Claire had a feeling life with Massie was about to get really exciting.